The End of the Web

Selver said hello three times in quick succession without any hope of a reasonable response: a fatal sense of curiosity stopped him from replacing the receiver and made him press it closer to his ear, as if that might help in picking up a clue about the mysterious caller.

On the other end of the line the silence was punctuated at first by the faint sound of breathing, then by the silvery chimes of a clock. The chimes were very much like those of his own old French clock. He was struck by the frightening idea that the telephone lunatic had somehow obtained access to the Welbeck Street Mews flat and made the recording in his own sitting-room. He suddenly shivered as though exposed to a chilling wind instead of midsummer heat. His heart vaulted as a Vox Humana voice read out what sounded like excerpts from references: "E should be your middle initial. Yes, E for efficiency. Highly pleased. Oh yes, indeed. Miracle worker! Your plan seems to have worked like a charm. No one else could have tidied the mess . . . tidied the mess . . . tidied the mess."

As the phrase was repeated mechanically a feeling of panic shot out of Leo Selver like a frightened horse with a kick and a sickening plunge that left him breathless, with a sharp pain in his side. He slammed down the receiver. He had practically forgotten what it was like to be really scared: during the war he had found it difficult to face up to terrors; now it seemed unbearable.

GEORGE SIMS

The End of the Web

WALKER AND COMPANY · NEW YORK

First published in the United States of America in 1976 by the
Walker Publishing Company, Inc.

This paperback edition first published in 1985.

ISBN: 0-8027-3137-6

Library of Congress Catalog Card Number: 75-32833

Printed in the United States of America

10 9 8 7 6 5 4 3 2 1

"For a moment Raskolnikoff had carefully watched his interlocutor's face, a face which continually caused him new astonishment. Although beautiful, it had points that were exceedingly unattractive. It might almost have been taken for a mask; the complexion was too bright, the lips too red, the beard too fair, the hair too thick, the eyes too blue, the gaze too rigid."

Dostoyevsky

Other titles in the Walker British Mystery Series

I

WOMEN! Everything about them fascinates me! The thought came into Leo Selver's mind so vividly that for a moment he felt that he had said it out loud. It was a naïve confession and not the kind of thing he wanted to admit. It was quickly pursued by a cynical comment from his other self: Seriously, though, there have to be worse ways of spending an afternoon.

Dichotomy: division or distribution into two parts; hence, a cutting into two; a division. He did contain two selves, dissimilar but complementary characters. There was the more obvious extrovert one, call him Leo for short, a typical Sun subject, born in August, romantic, impulsive, generous, greedy, vain, a man who made money quickly and lost it, philandered, played the fool, got into trouble. Then there was the subtler character, sober old Selver who had the second thoughts, watched everything and everybody including Leo, made sly comments and criticised, saw the absurdity of Leo's behaviour, tried to take evasive action whenever possible.

Judy Latimer was making a graceful exploration of Leo Selver's small sitting-room like a cat taken to a new home, at once inquisitive and wary. His flat was at the end of Welbeck Street Mews, a convenient situation that made it quiet and not overlooked. The sitting-room and kitchen faced the entrance of the mews: the bedroom and bathroom were at the back, and the only windows in those rooms were skylights.

Judy touched two paper-weights on the desk then turned towards Leo, using her greenish-blue eyes in an expressive way to show that she was enjoying herself.

"Fantastically quiet here! Why should it be so quiet?"

"It's a backwater of a backwater. There's not much traffic

7

in Welbeck Way, and then being tucked away from that."

Judy opened her eyes very wide in a bold expression that Leo found rather sexy though he knew it usually accompanied some criticism: "But you don't live here most of the time, do you? Someone in The Olive Branch said you lived in a country cottage."

Selver thought: So! You've been asking about me in my local. What do you want?—the whole picture?—that I've been married for twenty-six years, that we had a son who died when he was seven leaving us an inconsolable couple, that my wife had a hysterectomy a year later, that the operation which wasn't supposed to affect her sex life left her indifferent to it, that I've become a girl-chaser? He said: "That's right. A small cottage near Alton in Hampshire. Not all that distance from London but sometimes I work late at the shop and feel too tired to tackle the trip home."

"And your wife, doesn't she stay here?"

"Occasionally, when she comes to London to do some shopping, that kind of thing. She's having a few days by the sea at the moment."

Judy nodded significantly, conveying the thought: Aha! So that's why the mice can play. She turned away to continue her exploration, or was it a valuation survey?

Selver watched closely as she picked up an enamelled Arita jar then replaced it after a hasty glance and clambered on to the large leather couch to examine a small painting he had craftily hung above it.

Surely there could be few men who after consuming a good lunch and just too much wine would not experience some sexual stirring as Judy disclosed more and more leg. Leo was aware of only one handicap that prevented the situation being perfect: August 1973 was presenting another stifling hot day and a sexual wrestle would be less pleasant in such heat.

Leo was drawn to the couch nevertheless and sat down at the point furthest from her, closing his eyes for an instant listening to the Nat Cole disc spinning round in the bedroom.

8

It was an old favourite, *"Cherchez la femme"*:

> Look for the girl, monsieur,
> You're sure to find
> Clouds silver-lined
> Such is amour ...

Intoxication, the music, Judy's jonquil perfume, her visible charms and hints of those that were hidden, together with a faint sense of mystery about the girl, all contributed to Leo's sensual mood. Her skin looked as if it had been dusted with talcum powder then rubbed to achieve a silky smooth effect. He could imagine just how her long blonde hair would look falling over bare, satiny shoulders.

Leo steepled his fingers, looking as though he might be brooding on the world's problems, trying to dissemble his obsessional thoughts. The desire to touch Judy's skin was working in him like a fever, particularly now that he had only to reach out a few inches to fondle the back of her thigh, but he felt this was a game he had to play with skill. Disconcertingly Judy also seemed to contain two selves. He had thought so the first time he had seen her, only two weeks before this pleasant rendezvous, while having a lunch-time Guinness and sandwich in The Olive Branch, the nearest pub to his antique shop in Crawford Street. On that occasion she had been talking animatedly to a striking-looking Chinese girl. Watching them covertly, he had thought: If the Devil came in now I'd gladly strike up some kind of bargain with him, swapping a few of the fag-end years for the chance of an affair with either of those two beauties. A moment later, as if in quick response to his imaginary arrangement with Mephistopheles, Judy had smiled faintly in his direction, a gambit which had so surprised him that he had looked around to see if it had been intended for a younger or a better-looking man.

That meeting and two more in the same pub had shown her to be moody, at times appearing uninterested in him and

9

then suddenly switching back on, using her eyes to beckon with, holding the back of his wrist whenever she wanted to see the time. But now that another lunch-time meeting in The Olive Branch had led to her accepting his invitation to eat with him at the Hellenic in Thayer Street, now that she had been plied with good Greek food and wine, he felt quite uncertain as to the outcome of further proceedings.

"This I like. I mean very much. Really beautiful." Judy turned round with an awkward, rather tantalising movement showing even more leg, There had been a flash of white briefs and Leo's impulse was to kneel down and worship at the shrine of sex, kissing that delicious-looking bent knee.

But Selver noted the momentary business-like look in her eyes, just as if she was trying to get his weight in some deal. Without animated eyes and flashing teeth she looked rather cold and calculating. Perhaps she was the kind of girl with whom everything she touched turned to "sold".

Judy had removed the tiny Lucien Pissarro painting from the wall and seemed entranced by its jewel-like colours; her hands now formed an additional, possessive frame. Impulsively Leo, who placed little value on material possessions, having attended a thousand house-sales where all the hoarding of a lifetime was dispersed in a day, felt like offering it to her as a gift, but Selver was in control, as he was when it came to business, censoring the offer, saying nothing but nodding sagely.

Judy smiled mischievously and replaced the painting quickly, saying: "I feel rather guilty. I mean ... I must be holding you up, keeping you away from the shop. Expect you're busy."

"Dear girl, business deals for me are just necessary to bring about delightful moments like this. You see I've got my priorities right. Pleasure before business always."

It was Leo speaking and Selver thought: Listen to him. Another glimpse of underwear and he'll be singing "Love is my reason for living". But even Selver had to acknowledge

10

that the girl had a beautiful mouth, like that of the Michelangelo statue *Pietà*, her yellow hair shone and bounced with health, and her breasts looked high and perky.

Judy slid down on to the couch, turning round and lying back in one lithe movement. She said nothing but smiled enigmatically. She looked very relaxed and definitely seducible. Now was the time to cut out words and make some direct physical approach. Years ago he would not have hesitated but some vital confidence had ebbed away, leaving him at times in the unhappy position of a tyro in the arts of love.

Judy sighed, and even that slight movement of her breasts had a voluptuous appeal for Leo. She lifted her head, making a point that she was trying to catch the lyrics as Nat Cole sang "Let there be love".

"That's nice too. A golden oldie all right, but it's still good. And the piano."

"The pianist is George Shearing ..." Leo hesitated, realising that the name would probably mean nothing to her, wondering whether to add a few words about the brilliance of the blind pianist. Leo was so intent on gaining access to the girl's pearly belly and the secret mouth between her legs that his anxiety prevented him from thinking straight, and that would probably sabotage the operation. One part of his mind was foolishly acting like an advance scout, running on ahead of the present proceedings, warning him to remove his socks at the earliest opportunity, reminding him there were few less romantic images than a middle-aged man in pants and socks. All this elaboration and he had not yet touched the girl apart from putting his hand on her back as they left the restaurant.

"Oh dear—I just can't concentrate on the words. You gave me much too much wine. That was naughty! Now I'm feeling very vague. Everything is a bit unreal."

"Would you like to lie down in the bedroom for a while? It's cooler in there. Just a quiet lie-down and little cuddle perhaps. Nothing more than that."

11

"Next thing you'll be suggesting I take off my dress so it won't get creased." Judy smoothed the hem of her short blue shantung frock over her knees in a demonstration of modesty that was not really convincing.

"Well I'll have a bet with you that I shan't ask you to take off anything else. I just thought it would be nice to have a little lie-down in the cool, hold you in my arms for a while ..."

"I don't know ... Once I get horizontal ..."

"Don't be silly. You've got a will of iron."

"And you're a tricky character, that's for sure. Well, what's the bet?"

Again Selver was put off by her business-like expression, as if the bedroom decision depended solely on the size of the wager. For a moment he felt sure that this was not the first time she had put herself up for sale. She said she was a model but was vague about where she worked. Leo disliked the idea of paying directly for sex although quite willing to be generous about gifts. And the conversation was going on too long, practically turning into a debate. Obviously he should pull her off the couch and carry her into the bedroom, wrestle with her or smack her bottom, anything to make physical contact and achieve that happy position where words became superfluous. But the effect of the wine was passing off and his sexy mood was being replaced by one of tiredness. If the chat continued much longer his tone might become querulous. Selver mentally counselled himself to accept defeat: Ah well, it's all part of life's going-grey pattern. Give up, you fool, and let the girl go. Face the fact that she's not at all keen on this lying-down lark and pass off the situation with a joke.

As he was swallowing the toad of defeat, which encompassed sexual frustration and a deflated ego, his Trim-phone gave its preliminary note. At once he experienced a flicker of fear in case it was another of the subtly sinister anonymous calls: it reminded him vividly of the terrible risk he was taking under the pressure of that chancer, Sidney Chard. They were like men walking through a lions' den, with the deluding sensation of safety as long as the lions slept.

"Sorry, I'll have to take it. Might be a friend I was trying to contact this morning." He moved his head in the direction of the ringing phone.

"That's all right. Go ahead." Judy gave Leo a teasing kind of smile in which he thought he detected some affection. Had he been saved by the bell from giving up hope with her— was there still a chance of some lovers' games? He left the room momentarily buoyed up by this thought, but it had deserted him by the time he picked up the phone.

Once the toy-like receiver was off its stand there was an attention-focusing silence that made him realise this was not going to be an unusually welcome call from Sidney Chard, but another bizarre communication from Mr. Anonymous.

Selver said hello three times in quick succession without any hope of a reasonable response: a fatal sense of curiosity stopped him from replacing the receiver and made him press it closer to his ear, as if that might help in picking up a clue about the mysterious caller.

On the other end of the line the silence was punctuated at first by the faint sound of breathing, then by the silvery chimes of a clock. The chimes were very much like those of his own old French clock. He was struck by the frightening idea that the telephone lunatic had somehow obtained access to the Welbeck Street Mews flat and made the recording in his own sitting-room. He suddenly shivered as though exposed to a chilling wind instead of midsummer heat. His heart vaulted as a Vox Humana voice read out what sounded like excerpts from references: "E should be your middle initial. Yes, E for efficiency. Highly pleased. Oh yes, indeed. Miracle worker! Your plan seems to have worked like a charm. No one else could have tidied the mess ... tidied the mess ... tidied the mess."

As the phrase was repeated mechanically a feeling of panic

13

shot out of Leo Selver like a frightened horse with a kick and a sickening plunge that left him breathless, with a sharp pain in his side. He slammed down the receiver. He had practically forgotten what it was like to be really scared: during the war he had found it difficult to face up to terrors; now it seemed unbearable. He was long-suited on imaginative apprehension and short on guts—just the opposite type to Sidney Chard who appeared to revel in danger. So where was Sid now that he needed him?

Leo Selver's mind was a jumble of disconnected thoughts, and he knew that he could not continue immediately with the protracted seduction dialogue, but there was a chance that a pee and a quick wash might work wonders. He turned left instead of right on leaving the bedroom, walked a few paces along the corridor that led to the stairs down to the front door, and quietly locked himself into the bathroom. He turned on the cold tap hard to mask the sound of his peeing.

A flushed, exhausted face looked out at him from the mirror. "No fool like an old fool"; he spoke the cliché in a not quite natural voice, and saluted his mirror image ironically.

"Vivi pericolosamente." Standing by the lavatory, Selver remembered Mussolini's exhortation: "Live dangerously", looked down at his flaccid penis shrivelled by nerves, and laughed silently at himself. It was hard to believe that six months previously he had sometimes felt he might die of boredom because his life was so peaceful and uneventful. Each month then had appeared like the previous one, with only minute variations as to whether they were having dinner with friends or inviting them, making a buying expedition to York instead of Leamington Spa, and attending sales at Christie's rather than Sotheby's. All that had been altered in the course of a few days, and he had got the longed-for adventure. It was common enough to wish for a changed existence, but before embarking on dangerous escapades one

should consider whether one had the courage to face them out.

As Selver pulled the chain he said, "Yes, go on then, live dangerously!" in a quiet sneering voice. That fat buffoon Mussolini had provided an admirable tailpiece illustration to his own precept by appearing hung upside-down with Clara Petacci outside a petrol-station in Milan.

Cool down and calm down, Selver advised himself, filling the basin and splashing his face with cold water till the mirror presented a less hectic visage. He thought of Sidney Chard's motto, "Here goes nothing", to see if it had any magic left in it, and oddly enough found that he was feeling less panicky. Dare-devil Sid would think of some way of dealing with the worrying telephone business.

The door to the sitting-room was open wider than he had left it and Judy was no longer seated on the couch. Pushing the door right back, he found that the room was empty. The surprise brought back the sharp pain in his side. The silhouette of the standard-lamp blurred against the sun. The room became dark, almost black. It was an effort to make his legs work, as though he were following a dimly remembered pattern of behaviour. He took a few angry, excited steps at seeing a piece of paper propped up on the mantelpiece.

Dear Incorrigible,

Had to scoot—chance of a job and jobs are scarce just now!. Apologies—and thanks for the delicious lunch and the chatting up and everything! Long day tomorrow slaving in front of hot lights and cameras—I shall be in need of lots of wining and dining! Would you like to call round at my grotty pad in the evening, 8 p.m.? 14 Stephen Street, by the Gresse Buildings, off Tottenham Court Road. I like this quiet flat—and its tenant.

Not quite yours,

Judy

P.S. Shall not wait after 8.15 as I shall be starving!

The note had been written with Selver's black felt pen, though her light touch disguised this to a certain extent. Her writing was nervous, sharply pointed, and degenerated into scrawl at the end. He thought: I've taken another blow to the ego. Knowing that she "had to scoot", she could not have taken his suggestion about lying down seriously and was just teasing. So much for his seductive powers, so much for the charm of the older man!

He screwed up the note and threw it into the waste-paper basket, but it was an act of bluff, a mere pretence of independence. Tomorrow pathetic old Leo would be in Stephen Street at 8 p.m. sharp. He could have taken the pretence further and dramatically burnt Judy's message, as each word was engraved on his brain.

Walking back to the bedroom, Selver realised that coming face to face with yourself was sometimes an unpleasant experience that did not take place in front of a mirror. As he became older his attempts to seduce girls like Judy would become more and more ludicrous.

He removed the Trim-phone from its stand. The room was comparatively cool, and the clean sheets looked inviting. He sat down on the edge of the bed and took off his shoes and socks slowly like an old man. The pain in his side, which his mother would no doubt have classified as "a stitch", had moved a little and become duller, but he had a sensation of exhaustion as though he had not slept for several nights in a row. He was profoundly weary and a nap was essential before he again tackled the problem of finding Sidney Chard.

II

X FILE

SURNAME
CHARD

FORENAMES
SIDNEY ARTHUR

HOME ADDRESS
68 BEDFORD PLACE MANSIONS LONDON WC1

BUSINESS ADDRESS
CAMDEN PASSAGE ISLINGTON LONDON N1

BIRTH DATE
4 1 1918

NATIONALITY
BRITISH

PASSPORT NO

SMDW
X

MARITAL
STATUS

CREDIT R
X

CAR NO
MUX 121K

PROFESSION OCCUPATION
FURNITURE DEALER

BANK
LLOYDS

SPECIAL
CRIPPLE SMASHED LEFT KNEE CAP

CRIMINAL CODE
NONE

NOTES

Tough nut. Reputation of being
hard to deal with. Won the
Military Medal for bravery at
Monte Cassino serving with
Lancashire Fusiliers.
Watch this one.
Weakness – greed.

X FILE

SURNAME		FORENAMES	
SELVER		LEO FREDERICK	

HOME ADDRESS

BARN COTTAGE LASHAM ALTON HANTS

BUSINESS ADDRESS

CRAWFORD STREET LONDON W1

BIRTH DATE	NATIONALITY	PASSPORT NO
8 8 1923	BRITISH	

SMDW	CREDIT R	CAR NO
X MARITAL STATUS	X	TXU 242J

PROFESSION OCCUPATION	BANK
ANTIQUES DEALER	BARCLAYS

SPECIAL

STAYS SOME NIGHTS IN LONDON FLAT

CRIMINAL CODE

NONE

NOTES

Imaginative, soft, easy to
squeeze. Can be pressurised.
Has flat at 3a Welbeck Street
Mews - Ingersoll Lock.
Weakness - young women.

III

THE alarming ticking of a great clock which seemed to operate within himself awoke Leo Selver from his strange dream about a dead man. He started up in a cold sweat with no sensation of drowsiness, seeing everything about him with stereoscopic clarity, springing out of bed as though it were on fire. There was a panicky fluttering in his pulse, his heart was thudding wildly and had become the centre of the dull pain that had been in his side.

The vivid dream had been, as Sid would phrase it, "of your definitely superior type", for it had made continuous good sense without a single dip into absurdity, and seemed to enlarge his scanty knowledge of Lord Trewartha whom he had only known by studying old photographs and reading press cuttings. In the dream Lord Trewartha, who had been burnt to death at the age of sixty-five, was a young man again, a strong active man with a forceful personality, moving restlessly about his gaunt moorland house, laughing and talking cynically. Trewartha's conversation had been familiar and convincing, his taut face, leprechaun eyes and richly curved mouth had seemed more real than most dream characters. Equally disturbing and haunting, was the sound just before Selver had woken from the dream, the bleak sound of the wind blowing across the moors, a sound of emptiness at once calamitous and unredeemed.

The imaginary visit to the lonely moorland house had served to remind Selver that there was an incriminating piece of paper in one of his pockets. After dressing, he searched through all the clothes in his wardrobe. He never used a notebook or diary, but accumulated a collection of scraps of paper and card in his pockets, and these were usually only sorted out when his clothes were sent to be cleaned, and by then he had often forgotten the significance of dates and underlined reminders, and some of the names would be as meaningless as those on old cheque stubs.

After a few minutes he found the particular scrap he was anxious to destroy, filled with an elaborate doodle, the result of fiddling about with a ballpoint pen while taking a phone-call from Sidney Chard. It was a pattern rather like a spider's web embellished with tiny faces and pin-men equipped with balancing poles to tightrope walk on some of the linking lines. It also resembled a snakes-and-ladders board, but instead of penalties and short cuts there were the names Cuyp, Molyneux, Everard, Arkadie, Twelve Men's Moor and Trewartha. At the centre of the web he had written the ominous nickname Court-Card. Beneath the drawing there was a circle with a dot in it, which was interesting psychologically as it was the Boy Scout symbol for "I have gone home".

Selver burnt the drawing over the sink in his kitchen and flushed down the black fragments with considerable satisfaction, then let the cold water run on his wrists. The fluttering sensation in his pulse had stopped but the pain in his heart remained. He made another mental note to see his doctor, as he had done on half a dozen occasions in the past few months.

Some other scraps of paper he took into the sitting-room and placed on his blotter for a careful scrutiny. On a restaurant match-folder and on the back of a party invitation he had scribbled the name Buchanan. This name was repeated in red ink with the query Bathwick Mews? on a used envelope. Buchanan was a name that had been much in his mind during recent weeks. He could visualise certain circumstances in which it would be very helpful if he could call on the help of someone as tough as Eddy Buchanan, who had once held an amateur-boxing championship title and looked as strong as a bull. No doubt Sidney Chard considered that he was tough, and probably he had been in 1944, but a fifty-five-year-old cripple was deluding himself if he clung to that belief. For a while Selver had also considered trying to hire professional help and a private detective had seemed a possibility, but the idea had several drawbacks. Regarding Eddy Buchanan, it was absurd in a way to seek defence from someone for whom he had built sand-castles and given piggyback rides in the early 1950s, but the thin freckled youth of that epoch had turned into a raw-boned six-footer.

Selver had good reason to remember the last occasion on which he had seen young Eddy, for it had been at the funeral of Buchanan's parents who had both been fatally injured in a car crash. Attendance at the Golders Green Crematorium had been a sad occasion for Selver, a much sadder one for his wife Beatrice who had been very fond of Edna Buchanan, occasionally meeting her and corresponding from the time they had been neighbours in Hanbury Street, off the Whitechapel Road.

From the sombre midwinter funeral memories Selver's mind flitted back to happier days, the summers from 1948 to 1955, throughout his son Billy's lifetime in fact, when the Buchanans and the Selvers had shared holidays in Margate, Brighton and Weymouth. Money had always been short then and there had been little to spend on amusements apart from odd pennies for ice-creams. Five years older than Billy Selver, Eddy Buchanan had seemed to feel protective about him and was always willing to play with him on the beach while the parents went for walks. Selver knew that it was the sight of Eddy, healthy and happy, that had been the main reason for him wanting to move away from the Buchanans after Billy's death.

The address Bathwick Mews had stuck in his memory since the brief meeting at Golders Green. Eddy had said then that he could always be contacted there through a sports-car garage run by an ex-racing-driver friend of his. Selver knew that Eddy's own racing career had been brief. "Up like a rocket and down like the stick", he had once commented to Beatrice. Now Eddy might have resumed his feckless wanderings around Europe and be out of reach, but there was also a chance that he had settled down at last to some sensible job. Hovering tantalisingly in Selver's mind was the vague memory of more recent news of Eddy Buchanan, something that Beatrice had told him while he was occupied with other matters. For a few moments he fished around for this in his trivia-packed memory, then decided it was not worth worrying about when he could walk to Bathwick Mews in about five minutes from his shop in Crawford Street.

He decided on a useful time-table of events. Make one more telephone call to Sidney's home number; call in at Crawford Street; visit Bathwick Mews. He went into the bedroom again and dialled Sidney's number, visualising the slightly sombre and old-fashioned apartment, rather over-stuffed with "choice pieces". As the bell continued to ring without response the fleeting, absurd idea of a doublecross passed through his mind, then he heard a youthful voice sedulously repeating the number. Selver smiled and said: "All bets off."

"Hello, Uncle Leo."

"Hello, young Clive. Still sticking on seventeens?"

"That depends."

"I know it does. It depends on whether you can find a mug like me. I'm coming round for another pontoon lesson shortly. Meanwhile I'd like a word with your old man. I tried his shop this morning but they said he wouldn't be there today."

"He's not here, Uncle. Gone off on a business trip I think but I don't know where."

"Damn! Sorry Clive, but I was banking ... Is your mum in?"

"Gone shopping. She went to Harrods just after lunch. Be back by tea-time I expect."

"Okay Clive. Will you tell her I phoned and that I shall

call again, probably about six. Perhaps if she's popping out she'll leave a message with you where your dad is. I want to contact him pronto. What are you doing, old chap?"

"Just playing. Monopoly."

Selver knew it was ten to one that Clive was playing the game by himself and swallowed down the comment "Well, you should win then", saying: "Good. You need all the practice you can get. Because if your dad's coming home this evening I shall be calling in and we'll have a return match. For high stakes this time. I need to get back some of the cash I lost last week. Well, cheerio old lad."

"Can we play pontoon if there's not time for Monopoly?"

"Of course, Clive. Probably see you later on then."

"Good. Cheerio, Uncle Leo."

Clive's voice was too serious, his looks too thoughtful and his behaviour too circumspect for a boy of ten. Selver knew that being the only child of middle-aged parents was always liable to lead to a situation rather like that, but Norah and Sid had worked on the process of making Clive excessively well-behaved and above all passive. The Chards did not have the freemasonry and intimate ralationship of a happy family —they were more like three adults rooming together. In the busy, ambitious world that Norah and Sid inhabited a child was something of a handicap and they did not hide this, being quite open about their impatience to send Clive away to boarding-school.

Having replaced the phone Selver studied it as though it might perform a trick if left alone: he was unaware of his surroundings, brooding bitterly on the unfairness of life. When Billy had been alive he and Beatrice had found pleasure in his company every single day. Norah and Sidney Chard did not deserve to have Clive.

IV

A LUMP in the throat. Leo Selver was always puzzled by the mental and physiological processes which could contrive the painful sensation. This time it had been caused by seeing a boy about seven years old, dressed in grey trousers and a white shirt, waiting at the Belisha beacon on the corner of Paddington Street. Hearing children laughing or seeing them running homewards from school were the usual hazards. Tears pricked behind his eyes. He sniffed and swallowed.

Turning out of Marylebone High Street into Paddington Street, Selver realised he had walked from Welbeck Way "on automatic", oblivious of his surroundings, absorbed in his resentful thoughts about Billy's freak illness, the meningitis that had put a stop to any chance of real happiness for him with Beatrice. He felt sure that if Billy had lived their relationship would have been strong enough to make up for Beatrice's present sexual apathy. As it was he could not stop looking elsewhere, though he could see the folly of his behaviour. No doubt their mutual friends guessed at his affairs and thought Beatrice was wonderful to put up with his philandering. But would someone able to look deep into human hearts come to the same conclusion?

An unnatural posture compounded of things as trivial as sweating made him feel like an old man. He stopped walking, straightened up and looked at the sky. Usually a few days of such oppressive heat in England would bring a thunderstorm in its wake, but there was no sign of this happening. There were just a few widely spaced high white clouds in an azure sky. With luck he might have been looking at them now with Judy, watching them travel slowly across the skylight as they lay together. It was pillow talk of an intimate nature that Leo craved just as much as the sexual act.

24

"Hello, my dear. *Quo vadis*?" It was Professor H. Immanuel Klein gravely raising his homburg hat to Leo Selver as if to a passing funeral.

"Hello, Manny. Just going back to the shop. Did you want to see me?"

"Yes, my dear. I've something to show you. Perhaps— here? I've been to your shop once already and walking the streets today ... This heat ..."

Klein made an irritable grabbing movement as if removing an invisible fly from the air. He had made no compromise in his clothing to deal with a temperature in the eighties, wearing his usual heavy, navy three-piece suit. Klein had been a Professor of Semantics at Frankfurt till 1933 and since then had followed various occupations, ending up as a fairly successful "kitchen table" dealer in antiques. He spent two or three days of each week in visiting remote country junk shops searching for things he could sell to West End dealers. His bulky brief-case always contained the current *ABC Rail Guide*, and he could rattle off the best morning trains for Canterbury, Yarmouth and Yeovil. He lived in the basement flat of a gloomy house in Westbourne Grove, immured by a broken doorbell and increasing deafness. His rooms had grimy ceilings, and walls covered with fading photographs in crumbling frames. He owned a gramophone that did not work, a pile of antique opera records in dusty brown paper covers, and an equally old wireless set that had started to blare out again after a decade of silence. In his flat there were no newspapers, magazines or television: its atmosphere had stuck in the 1930s, while a desk calendar remained fixed at 22.10.41. He was known variously in the trade as "Manny", "the Prof", and "that fucking know-all Klein".

Klein began to laboriously undo the various straps and locks which guarded his heavy hide case. He breathed heavily at the effort and Selver longed to curtail the performance by helping him, but knew from experience that this would not be welcome. Klein's sensitive mouth and pebble glasses were surrounded by a beard of bristly black and white whiskers. Behind the thick lenses there were pale, wise, opaque eyes. He kept on fiddling with an intransigent buckle, but scrutinised Selver's face like a jeweller examining a watch. His lips moved silently, as if he was working out a problem. A biscuit crumb trembled on one wiry white whisker. Selver looked at him admiringly, thinking that he could not imagine the circumstances in which Klein would lose his natural dignity. He remembered the hectic, nervous face reflected in the bathroom mirror and thought: Christ, I've lost any chance of dignity myself by telling too many lies and acting so deviously. What a strange life I've made for myself. What a web we weave indeed.

Klein gave Selver a searching look and said: "You worry me, my dear. Lately you've changed. It's like talking to a different man."

Selver smiled unnaturally, unable to think of a reply.

"Always in a hurry, rushing here, there and everywhere. Whenever I call at your shop they say you're out and usually they don't seem to know where you are. It's not like the old days. And what's this I hear about a move? Davies Street? Can that be true?"

"A possibility. No more than that. I've been to see some premises there. It's strictly *comme ci comme ça* at the moment."

Klein had given up struggling with the tight strap as though it presented an insoluble problem; he leant back heavily against the wall of the small public garden.

"Surely—such premises—would they not be very expensive, my dear? And the rates there, what kind of rates must they pay next door to Claridge's?" Klein looked apprehensive suddenly, struck by a troublesome thought. "You're not thinking of a partnership with your friend Mr. Chard?"

Selver was able to laugh spontaneously. "Good God no. Not a chance in a thousand. Sid would hate that as much as I would." He wanted to reassure the old man, knowing Klein's

26

deep-seated dislike of Sidney Chard. "My only possible change will be a short move—only a few streets away—*if* I make it. Nothing else. Just the same old set-up. You'll keep on finding me nice things and I shall keep on buying them."

"So you say, and you probably mean it now. But molehills can become mountains, if you see what I mean." Klein's tone was becoming general and discursive which usually Selver welcomed and found instructive, but it was a different matter when standing sweating in the glare of the sun.

"For instance, my dear," Klein paused, obviously reaching out for facts to fit a theory, "example given—in 1905 an obscure young man, only a Technical Officer, Third Class, in the Swiss Patent Office, submitted four brief articles to the *Annalen der Physik*. Hardly noticed at the time, they were to bring radical changes in man's view of the world. I refer, of course, to Albert Einstein."

"Oh really, Manny! Come on! The connection eludes me. An Einstein I'm not."

"My dear, I was only trying to explain ... that I've trained myself to observe all changes and other factors—things going on about me—and try to foresee what may develop. Every time I see you at a sale now you're talking away to Mr. Chard. Like conspirators! Then I hear of the expensive move. It's ambitious, very ambitious. Out of character, if I may be so bold. So I think perhaps it's going to be Chard & Selver Ltd."

"He won't listen to me!" Selver appealed to an invisible audience. "What do you do when your old friend won't believe you?" He had felt increasingly uneasy as Klein made his prediction: in a way it came much closer to the truth than he liked. It was comparable to having your hand read by a gipsy who turned out to have an insight into traits you preferred to keep secret. The myopic old man with failing hearing appeared to be a poor observer. In fact, immune to many general interests, with a marked distaste for politics and sport, he was in a good position to concentrate his thinking only on people

27

and *objets d'art*, as if bringing them into crucial focus under a microscope.

Klein muttered something in German, nodding his head. "Yes, quite a combination! Your taste and flair together with that man's drive and ambition. I have to admit, though, that I should not welcome it personally. You know he would not be pleased for me ..."

"Tears!" Selver pointed to his eyes dramatically: he knew the old boy liked a joky approach. "I shall be crying soon if you won't listen. No, repeat no, partnership is in the offing."

Klein undid the last strap and reached into his capacious bag, pulling out a vase-shaped object wrapped up in blue tissue-paper which he slowly undid to reveal white tissue-paper. He said: "Something unusual. As soon as I saw it I thought it would appeal to you."

Selver had foolishly run out of patience. "May I?" he said, reaching out to take the tissue-paper parcel.

Klein held on to it firmly, saying: "No. If you won't listen to the sales talk you can't buy the piece."

"Now he wants me to change the habits of a lifetime and be patient."

The white tissue-paper was teased off slowly as Klein muttered "Something special" and made one of his more or less tactile acts of cognition with the mysterious object, then held up a silver hare's head very close before his eyes.

Selver touched the finely modelled ears of the hare. "A stirrup cup. Rare like that. The foxhead cups are comparatively common. No base, but that's the original state. It was handed full to the mounted rider who held it by the fox's muzzle or the hare's ears as he drank. About 1800 I should say."

Klein savoured the moment as if a secret diagnosis had been confirmed. "I didn't know ... You see I took a chance and paid quite a sum. I thought you would like it."

"I do like it." Selver took hold of the cup and looked at it closely. "1809. Made by Ermes and Barnard." He rolled his

28

eyes in a comical fashion and did an imitation of a Cockney "kitchen table" dealer which he knew would amuse Klein: "Well, Sir, that's your veritable picturesque! What an item! Oh quite unique! The old party what sold it to me was heartbroken to part with it! Nothing else quite like it in Lunnon, Sir!" He continued to examine it carefully as he spoke. "You see these words engraved round the rim? A toast to a hunt in the Forest of Bowland. Yes, this is rare as well as attractive —haven't had one like it before. Can you leave it with me for a few days, Manny, and we'll work out a good price?"

"Of course, my dear. But you appreciate I couldn't come to such an arrangement with your friend Mr. Chard."

"No, perhaps not. Well, you know Sid. He's a bit short on tact."

"No tact. No sense of occasion. No ... Well of course it's all a game, this business of dealing, but even a game has to have some rules ..."

"Yes, of course." Selver was anxious to cut short this analysis of Sidney Chard's character. "Got time for a cup of char?"

"Not today, my dear, though it is nice of you to ask me. I want to get home now. My feet ache. This heat ..."

"Okay then, Manny, we'll leave it like that. Many thanks for offering me this piece. I'll be in touch." Selver walked off, holding the stirrup cup casually by one of the hare's ears. His pleasure in such things had once been genuine but had fallen away during the years and now was largely feigned, just part of his professional approach. He turned once to wave to the old man and walked on briskly as if he was looking forward to returning to his shop, though in fact the prospect of an afternoon of business was as dull as an evening of his own company. It was strange how the strong conceit of I, I, I always led one forward.

Selver was again oblivious of his familiar surroundings. He was looking into his future and finding it bleak. Propped up by the redoubtable Sidney Chard M.M., he would no doubt survive the tricky, dangerous next few weeks; he would become wealthier and this would lead to more success in his business; he would achieve his move to Davies Street and a few remaining ambitions of that kind. There would be Judy and later on other girls like Judy, none of whom would give a damn for him, and it would all be empty, empty, empty.

He remembered his foolish excitement, like that of a love-sick youth, on looking into Judy's greenish-blue eyes while her sharp-nailed fingers held his wrist. On two occasions she had made quite a performance of doing this while she looked at his watch, and he had found her faintly possessive air in these flirtatious moments very pleasurable. Knowing how stupid he was to persist with an affair with a girl half his age, yet there was nothing else he looked forward to apart from the proposed meeting in Stephen Street.

He moved his wrist-watch and mentally dictated a résumé of his position: Dear psychiatrist. Well, here I am at fifty. From here on it is downhill all the way. No beliefs, no causes attract me. So what's the prognosis, doc? Obsessional Oedipus complex? The Albertine syndrome?

Selver realised he had spoken the last word out loud, inadvertently, and looked round to see if any passer-by had noticed. This made him feel foolish and even hotter than before. Sweating in the glaring sunlight at the Baker Street crossing, waiting for the traffic signals to change colour, he thought in a moment of rare detachment: The cause of most of my troubles has been my inability to deny myself anything.

V

THE man wearing white cotton gloves had a mind made sick and blind by the past. He was ruled by an *idée fixe*: the con-

30

stant necessity for imposing a pattern upon chaos. This day-time obsession was coupled with an ever-recurring dream of a ruthless hand-to-hand fight for existence in which he just managed to survive. The dream had a hundred variations but the central theme was always that of obtaining a superior position in the bloody struggle by forethought and planning.

The man straightening the fingers of the white cotton gloves thought of himself as X. In his wallet, along with a dozen other press-cuttings which he considered of particular significance, he always carried one with the headline THE UNKNOWN FACTOR x. In the equation let X equal the unknown factor: X stood for unrivalled strength, meticulous planning and all-round efficiency. X always felt intensely alone, as if he was the only man alive in a world otherwise peopled by phantoms.

The man using white-gloved fingers to open a black leather brief-case stood in the shadow of a derelict cottage in the Chilterns. A cottage without a name at the edge of a wood known as the Oaken Grove. A pathway, which would be muddy in winter but now was of bone-dry clay along which a car could be driven with care, led from the cottage along the edge of the wood to a farm gate where it joined another path leading through the Oaken Grove and a rough track that ran down to the A4155 road connecting Marlow and Henley.

For three weeks X had quartered the Home Counties with a mental list of requirements which he could not put to any house agent, namely: (1) deserted house or cottage yet one not obviously tumble-down; (2) secluded site; (3) reasonably easy access by car; (4) privacy; (5) deep pond within short distance.

The nameless cottage by the Oaken Grove which looked as if it must have housed a gamekeeper earlier in the century filled all these requirements. Most of the tiles on the roof were intact at the front of the cottage though they had given way at the back: all the front window-frames were still present and X had hung up grimy net curtains so that from twenty feet the cottage looked inhabited. The seclusion and privacy were all that could be hoped for, with no person living within a mile. The track from the A4155 was steep and stony, but negotiable by car. A winter stream ran through the wood, feeding a pond at what had been the end of the cottage garden; the pond was ten feet deep with black, stagnant water, covered in duckweed.

X re-checked the contents of the brief-case which he had laid on the ground-elder-covered path at the side of the cottage. The case contained a replica Frontier Colt revolver, a facsimile so exact that it would escape detection unless it was examined closely; a roll of wire, wire-cutters and pliers; a tin of plasters; a papier-mâché mask. In purchasing the mask X had appeared to be casual in the shop, as if buying it was a caprice, but he had studied the selection with care. It was the most natural one he could find, so that from a distance it did look like a face. A hideous yellow or grey one made to put on a Guy Fawkes' dummy might appear to be more frightening, but the nearly normal visage had a subtlety about it that appealed to X. Years before, in the orphanage, he had been frightened by a boy in a similar mask, and that was the kind of thing he never forgot.

X straightened up from his examination of the vital equipment. He cast an exact shadow on the sunlit path. The early morning mist had changed to a flimsy cloud flotilla vanishing to the north and leaving behind it a clear blue sky. X was tempted to explore the derelict cottage once more. He liked the walls from which layers of varicoloured papers had come unstuck to reveal damp patches and fungus; the wavy brick floor decorated with moss and grimy streaks of bird-droppings; the gaping chimney in the tiny living-room; the brambles and nettles that flourished by the walls; the flagstones in the kitchen fringed with knot-grass; the pervasive smell of decay. X stared in through a window at the dank kitchen: he had left the side door to it open to facilitate immediate access when his hands would be full.

X looked at his watch. It was 8.55 a.m. and there were only

five minutes to pass before Mr. Sidney Chard was due for his appointment. Having studied Chard's character he did not expect him to be late. Indeed X would have been willing to take a bet and give good odds that Chard would both be punctual and stick to the agreement of coming alone; Chard was an extreme individualist with a high opinion of his ability to deal with anything that came his way. Of course, X had to be prepared for the other possibility even though it was remote; if there was someone else with Chard, X had prepared a simple alternative scenario: one in which he would disappear as soon as the car with two passengers came into sight, climbing under the wire fence into the wood and making his way down through the Oaken Grove to the spot where he had hidden his Volkswagen, just off the road leading to Marlow.

8.58 a.m. on Wednesday the 15th of August 1973. No doubt Chard considered this was likely to be an important day in his life; but he did not realise that it was one of vital importance, more eventful even than the day in 1944 when Corporal Sidney Chard of the Lancashire Fusiliers had led an attack on Point 445, a German outpost in front of the Monastery Hill at Cassino. X had studied an account of the battle and knew that Chard had been awarded the Military Medal for his bravery in a hand-to-hand fight during which he had been wounded in the knee by a bullet from an M.G. 42. Qualm: a sensation of fear and uneasiness. In tackling a man like Chard, "fearless and resourceful", one was bound to take a risk. The best plans could go wrong. Quarry: to prey or feed, to hunt down. X was attracted by words that began with a Q and could rattle off dictionary definitions of half a dozen which had a particular significance for him.

9.00 a.m. A khaki-coloured robin watched X with beady eyes. X watched an orb spider that had strung its large web in a corner of the ramshackle front-door porch. X was fascinated by spiders and knew a good deal about them, including the superstition that spiders are fond of music because they become excited when a musical instrument sets a web trembling. A particularly interesting fact was their ability, while making sticky spirals to catch their prey, to spin dry radial threads on which to approach the victims. The common garden spider sat at the centre of its web waiting for an insect to get caught in the sticky drops on the spiral threads. X waited, with sticky spirals and dry radials all prepared, concealed by the old wooden porch, to spy upon Sidney Chard's approach.

Outwardly calm, X was the subject of extreme excitement: he knew that in the next half-hour he was going to live more intensely than most men did in twenty years. His body was preparing for the vital trial of strength, his mind concentrated absolutely on a ritualistic series of movements which he had visualised and rehearsed.

Down the track there was the sound of a powerful engine: a moment later X saw Chard's green Rover 3500 effortlessly mounting the steep track. X bent down and adjusted the papier-mâché mask over his face. He had made the eye slots larger so that his vision was not impaired. He picked up the large Colt in his right hand and held it behind his back.

The driver of the Rover stopped as near as possible to the farm gate and sounded the horn. A moment later he got out of the car awkwardly and leant on an ash-stick as he opened the gate, staring towards the cottage and calling out in an irritable voice: "Hello! Hello there! Mr. Quentin? Are you there?"

X moved away from the porch but stood under a low branch of an elm-tree which he knew would keep him partly concealed. He held his left arm out in front of his face and waved to Chard but made no move towards him.

Chard said: "Oh, good. I thought for a moment ..." He began to walk up the path towards the cottage laboriously. "So you are here. Well, I'm on time as agreed. I hope all this business is going to be worth my while."

X said: "Yes", quietly. The mask made the word come

34

out slurred and sounding funny. He still held his left arm up as if welcoming the crippled man. When Chard was within twenty feet X dropped his left arm and produced his revolver, pointing it straight at Chard's chest and walking forward quickly, saying: "Stand still!" The command came out as "Shtand shtill!"

Chard did as he was told. X had banked on him having a healthy respect for firearms as did most ex-servicemen who had seen action. Chard's face was suddenly pale. He said, "For fuck's sake. What's this? A bad joke?"

"Not a joke."

"Christ!"

Chard had melancholy brown eyes, black hair that had thinned and retreated from a widow's peak, and an aggressive Punch-like chin. He had heavy shoulders and a wide chest. He stared at the Colt as though hypnotised by it, repeating the words "You fool, you fucking fool" to himself. His right hand slid a few inches down the shaft of the stick.

X said: "Keep quite shtill. Give me the shtick. The shtick! I want it."

Chard took his eyes off the Colt and said: "Wait! For Christ's sake let's talk. Give me a chance."

X nodded. "Yesh. I'll give you a chance. But first give me the shtick." Immediately the stick was in his left hand he lashed out with it at Chard's legs. Chard lunged forward desperately with his right fist and then toppled over. X rained down swingeing blows. A particularly vicious blow on Chard's chest made him jerk forward, crying out something incomprehensible. A denture fell out of Chard's mouth, leaving him with a long sunken upper lip. The sound of breath from his half-paralysed diaphragm was like an eerie, continuing sigh. A blow on his neck made him twist about convulsively from side to side. When X paused for a moment Chard fumbled with a button, letting out a captive cry: "Oh Jesus, Jesus!"

X ripped off his mask with the hand that held the Colt and rained down more blows with the stick, a series of methodical strokes which he punctuated by talking in a quiet persuasive voice: "Look old man ... Mr. Quentin speaking ... What we'll do ... Is this ... We'll take it slowly ... That's right ... Easy does it."

After a few minutes X crouched down on his haunches by the inert body. The only sounds to be heard were his own rapid breathing, a blackbird singing in a may-bush, and the insistent trilling of larks high above the meadow. X was sweating profusely as he stooped to pick up the denture and place it in Chard's inside jacket pocket; he then surveyed the ground around the body with minute care as if he were a detective scrutinising the scene. Some blood mixed with vomit had run down Chard's jacket and shirt but there did not appear to be a trace of it on the grass. In threshing about convulsively Chard had broken some stalks in a patch of ground-elder.

X kept his attention fixed on the blood-stained jacket as he dragged the heavy body to the cottage, then went back to pick up the stick, mask and revolver. He covered the flag-stones in the kitchen with some old newspapers and laid the body on them. He went through all of Chard's pockets, removing a bulging wallet, a diary and an envelope. He then covered Chard's gaping mouth with plaster and bound his wrists and ankles with wire. Following his ritualistic plan he ran wires along the body and tightened them so that in the end he had transformed the intractable corpse into a box-like structure.

Glancing down at the Colt as he went out of the kitchen door X noticed a streak of blood along the barrel, which was perplexing for he could have sworn that he had not used it in the assault. With this vivid reminder of the scrupulous care that was essential, he concentrated his gaze upon the ground as he retraced his steps to the scene of the hand-to-hand struggle and then on to the car.

Driving the Rover to the cottage was accomplished in a few moments without any difficulty, then X placed the body together with the stick, mask and revolver in the boot. As an afterthought he collected the old newspapers from the kitchen floor and laid them over the corpse, then locked the boot.

As he turned the ignition key and the V8 engine purred in response, X was aware of a sudden tight feeling in his chest: the drive along the overgrown kitchen garden path through briars and great mounds of couch-grass would be more difficult in a large car than it had been during his trial run in the Volkswagen. He moved the gear lever to the lowest drive position and eased off the hand-brake. The Rover moved slowly forward, gliding smoothly over the bumpy path, but a long briar forced its way through an open window, inducing in X a momentary sensation of panic. He stopped the car and wound up all the windows tight before proceeding again. He could not entirely avoid the grey lichen-covered branches of the deformed apple-trees. They scraped the windows and top of the car, screeching a series of protests as though making up for the fact that Chard had died without a scream or a whimper. One tough branch was particularly intransigent, being bent back rather than broken and then whipping against the top of the car with a bang that made X break out again in a cold sweat. By the time the Rover was near to the pond X's hands were wet and shaking.

When X stepped from the Rover, switching off the engine and setting the hand-brake rather too hard with a nervous jerk, he experienced a profound feeling of relief at having successfully negotiated the drive to the pond. He had no mechanical knowledge of cars, and one recurring doubt about his plan had been possible trouble with the Rover's automatic drive.

He felt calm again and once more master of the situation as he stood at the edge of the pond surveying its weed-choked surface. The pond was partly screened by may-bushes but he looked beyond them to scan the large meadow and the distant woods, straining his eyes to detect any sign of movement.

He could hear the faint sound of a tractor's engine a long way off, but he could see nothing to worry about.

He walked back to the Rover slowly, going over all that had happened in his mind, thinking hard whether he had made any slips that could be detected. He looked round the interior of the car to make sure that there was nothing that might float out when the vehicle was submerged, then locked the two glove-compartments. After locking the cap to the petrol-tank he tried the boot again, then replaced the key in the ignition, set the gear lever at neutral and released the hand-brake.

Pushing the Rover into the pond was an easier job than he had imagined. Once he had got the heavy car in motion it slid forward and vanished into the water with movements that were like a convulsive series of gigantic belches. X had to step back sharply to avoid a spray of mud and weed. Large bubbles continued to rise for a few minutes with a reek of stagnation, then the surface was still again. There was a square area free of weed but half an hour would change that.

X picked up the largest branch broken from one of the apple-trees and used it to obliterate the car's tracks through the couch-grass and cow-parsley. He collected the other broken branches and twigs and threw them into the thick undergrowth. Entering the cottage, he took off his white cotton gloves and put them with his other equipment in the brief-case. Then he began to walk down the path, keeping his eyes on the ground as he again retraced the route that he had taken with Sidney Chard. He examined the patch of ground-elder closely and decided it would have taken Sherlock Holmes to prove that the broken stalks were not the result of lovers lying there. Once out of the shade of the elm-trees he was aware of the larks singing high above and the growing warmth of the sun on his back. It was going to be a hot day as well as a very busy one for X.

VI

A ZINC-COLOURED sky with a galvanised-iron horizon. Leo Selver stood on the steps of a Cypriot restaurant in Charlotte Street looking at the sky and taking deep breaths as he waited for Judy Latimer to "spend a penny" in the basement toilet. After a stiflingly hot day the oppressiveness of the evening of Wednesday the 15th August, 1973, was extreme. Selver felt sure that a thunderstorm must develop soon and welcomed the idea of cooling rain. Over in the south the grey sky had an ominously bruised look about it. All day he had been the subject of a mild but persistent headache which he partly blamed on the sweltering heat. It seemed as if London had been temporarily transformed into a vast oven, or an experimental chamber from which the air was being extracted. He said, "Can't breathe properly", to himself in a mock whining tone and then laughed at the idea of putting this to Judy as an excuse for an unsatisfactory sexual performance; he had an unpleasant premonition that the evening might end or the night be punctuated with some kind of apology for impotence. After wanting the girl so badly, now that the sexual act seemed a definite possibility he had no desire at all.

Leo Selver was puzzled by his curious invalid eunuch-like state, for on other occasions the chance to make love to an attractive woman had always found him ready and cancelled out minor aches and pains. His evening with Judy had started off badly, somehow getting him on the wrong foot, and he had not been able to recover his balance. On meeting her outside a shabby house at the end of a demolished row in Stephen Street she had come into his arms as if that was the natural thing to do, and her manner had been quite the reverse of the teasing one she had adopted in his flat. He had found her open-mouthed kiss and probing tongue sweet but surfeiting, like a mango, and the image of the fruit lingered on in his mind after their embrace was over—the rich, juicy yellow flesh, so much of it, and of such cloying quality.

Judy's appearance had been as much of a surprise to him as her behaviour: her make-up was much more extreme than on the other times they had met, and she was dressed in an abbreviated version of a French sailor's jersey that left her midriff bare, and white hipster trousers that barely concealed her navel. The clinging jersey revealed her figure to be fuller than he had thought and as they had walked to Charlotte Street she had held his arm lightly one moment, clinging tight the next, pulling him into contact with her breast in a provocative fashion. He could hardly believe she was the same girl who had been so reluctant to lie down on his bed.

"Darling, that meal was simply delicious."

Selver looked down the basement steps to see Judy coming up. He felt that he had a sheepish smile glued to his lips: perversely he wanted the evening to be over and done with; he realised how pleasant it would be to be spending it in Beatrice's undemanding company, walking along the front at Brighton where the sea-breezes would blow away his headache and he would not be expected to excel at sexual athletics.

As Judy reached the top of the steps she put her hands on Selver's shoulders and kissed him on the lips, saying immediately afterwards: "God, I hope that wasn't terribly garlicky!"

"No, of course not. I had the *humous* too."

"So you did, darling. Wait a sec. I absolutely insist on you removing your jacket. Poor chap, you looked terribly warm in there. Let me." She undid the jacket and helped him take it off, then quickly removed his tie, folded it up and put it in his pocket.

"No point in looking super-smart in such weather. Besides, you're very dishy in just a shirt."

Judy's fingers closed round his wrist as they began to walk along Charlotte Street. Her face was pleasantly flushed and

40

her eyes shone with excitement. Her honeysuckle scent seemed to be compounded with some other warm odour from her skin that Leo found enticing even in his strangely lack-lustre mood.

As Judy chattered on about the restaurant which she had chosen for their dinner, Selver was trying to understand her changed attitude towards him. Throughout the meal she had ignored the handsome young waiters who had hovered round their table even though one had tried to catch her eyes, laughed extravagantly at Selver's few feeble jokes, touched his hand at intervals between a great deal of eating and drinking. Leo had been very conscious of the insistent warm pressure of her leg against his while he toyed with his plate of *humous*, hiding the remains of it with a knife and fork when she cleaned her plate. Afterwards he had picked at a lamb kebab while she devoured a large helping of roast suckling pig, then patiently sipped a weak mixture of wine and water when she surprisingly ordered a dish of fried *calamares* instead of a sweet. She had drunk three-quarters of a bottle of *retsina* and most of the red wine. Swaying to the *bouzouki* music, she had gently kicked his foot from time to time and once had trodden on it quite firmly, all the time looking into his eyes and smiling enigmatically.

Selver thought: My ESP is trying to tell me something. Perhaps she is what is known in modern parlance as a "cock-teaser", perhaps she's trying really hard to get me in the mood again before running off as she did the other day. Perhaps she really hates men.

"Leo ..." Judy stared at Selver when they reached the corner of Percy Street. "Is it okay if we have another drink before we go back to my place?"

"We are going there then?"

"We most certainly are. Poor darling. You ... I shan't be doing another Cinderella trick if that's what you think. Wait a mo. Here's another garlicky taste so that you'll know." Judy clung tight as they kissed so that Leo was aware of every

41

inch of her body, but it had as much effect on him as embracing a statue.

"See what I mean? No, it's just that—well, my flat's a slightly grotty dump. Another drink or two and we shall be unaware of the grottiness."

"We could go on to Welbeck Street if you like."

"Definitely not, love. It's just round the corner and I'm probably exaggerating the grottiness. Anyway, tonight it's my turn to entertain you. Besides it'll be good for you to see how the other half lives. You may not get many more chances. Condemned premises you see! You must have noticed the other houses in the street are down."

"Not Gresse Buildings."

"Quite right. Not Gresse Buildings. They will remain in Stephen Street as a reminder of ... well—of something. But my old house is definitely for the chop. That's why I got the ground-floor flat at a knockdown bargain price. The upstairs part's already vacant. And my six months is nearly up."

"What will you do then?"

"Don't know, love." Judy looked at him with a serious expression for a moment, then she shrugged. "I don't plan much. And that's a fact. Well, it's not much good, is it? Yes, to sum up—my advice folks is, don't plan much. Now, where was I? Suggesting a drink at the Bricklayer's, was I not?"

"What's that?"

"Just one of your nice old-fashioned-type pubs, The Bricklayer's Arms in Gresse Street. We have to pass the door walking to my place anyway. A good ambience there, as they say, this time of night. Okay?"

For a moment Selver was tempted to tell her that he would much prefer to have some coffee. He wanted to say: "Let's just talk and forget the Romeo bit. Tell me about your plans that didn't come off. I am interested." But his ubiquitous pride prevented this. He said "Fine" and accompanied her like a sleep-walker.

The dark sky was lit by a distant flash of lightning followed by a rumble of thunder when they reached the corner of Rathbone Place and Gresse Street.

Judy said, "Just made it in the nick of time. Here we are."

The Bricklayer's Arms was jam-packed with a mostly young, modishly dressed crowd. Judy seemed to know quite a few of its patrons but she cut short their greetings, pushing her way to the bar, saying: "I'd love a vodka, darling. But you'll have to push and shout a bit. I'll hold your jacket."

Selver moved further along the bar to get within reaching distance of the blonde barmaid who was being kept extremely busy. He stood next to a tall young man with a mop of black curls who was saying to his companion: "Well you can tell Trevor this. I'm putting the balance-sheet through the computer and if it as much as coughs I'll have his guts for garters."

Selver ordered a large vodka, and some tonic water with a slice of lemon, planning to say the tonic was gin if questioned by Judy. He pondered what it was that prevented him from telling her that he did not feel up to consuming any more alcohol or embarking on love-making. He could not believe that impotence had really set in at fifty. Worrying all day because he could not contact Sidney Chard might have something to do with his malaise. Then again, he had been disappointed on going to Bathwick Mews to find that Eddy Buchanan was off on his travels, this time in Greece or the Greek Islands. It had been a prime example of a drowning man grasping at a straw to think of contacting Buchanan—how ironic that he should try to seek assistance from someone he had once verbally run down, talking to Beatrice about "young Eddy's self-destructive, feckless existence". These must be the reasons why he felt so down and incapable of responding to Judy. But perhaps middle age had something to do with it too. Selver thought: Life is an obstacle race with most of the obstacles grouped at the far end.

Making slow progress, carrying the glasses high to prevent

them being spilled, Selver reached a position two or three feet from Judy, but his way was barred by a wall of tightly packed bodies. He thought he heard her saying to another young, exotically dressed girl: "As useless as a spare prick." He was disconcerted by this but the next moment she seemed to give him a sincere smile as she took her drink, grinning attractively after the first sip: "Werry good wodka. Is not Russian wodka. Is not even Polish wodka. Is ..."

"Good evening, Miss Latimer." A tall, young man grinned down mockingly at Judy.

"Good evening, Mr. Crest." The mock formality of the exchange seemed in an odd way to hint at a close intimacy. Judy followed it up by saying: "Leo—this is Toby Crest. Toby—Leo Selver."

Crest said: "Hello. What a crush! How does one get a drink here? Send up smoke signals? Damn! I could do with a pint."

Selver said: "Then I'll get it. I'm nearer. A pint of what?"

"That's very kind. Best bitter. Thank you."

Selver welcomed the chance to move up to the bar again as he was interested to see what would develop between Judy and the young man. Crest was over six foot tall with the spare build of an athlete. He had long blond hair and a deeply tanned face. He wore a damson-coloured shirt with smoke-blue trousers. A silver bracelet dangled from one brown wrist. A square chin and a sharply cut mouth with a ruthless expression killed any hint of effeminacy. Crest's long green eyes, fringed with dark lashes, scanned the bar quickly as if to see whether there were any better possibilities than Judy. There was the definite air of a Flashman character about him. Selver thought: How nice to be young and casual, with such an air of independence. He ordered a pint of bitter and another large vodka but deliberately made slow progress edging back, giving the young couple an opportunity to talk by themselves, thinking that this chance meeting with Toby Crest might provide a way out of an embarrassing situation.

44

Pushing round an eighteen-stone character who dominated a section of the bar-counter, Selver found that Judy and Toby were indeed engrossed in conversation though it did not appear to be of a flirtatious nature; they both looked serious and thoughtful. They stopped talking as he came close, and Judy reached out for her second vodka. Crest took the pint of beer while fumbling in his pocket, saying: "You're sure I can't pay for these?"

Selver shook his head, smiling. He felt very detached, even remote. Just for once he did not want to win the girl. Looking at Crest's smooth brown skin and lustrous blond hair he mentally compared them with his own. Largely owing to Sidney Chard's devious machinations he had gone without a summer holiday, and his own face was pale and lined. Obviously Judy would prefer to spend the night with Crest. He decided that he would aid any such possibility; he fancied the idea of turning right instead of left on leaving the pub, making his solitary way back to Welbeck Street, taking some aspirin, followed by a bath and bed.

Judy and Toby seemed to be in some competition as to how quickly they could dispose of their drinks. The pint of bitter vanished and Toby said: "Very good drop of beer that. But this place is famous for its bitter. Can I buy a round before I push off?"

Selver was surprised to see that Judy absorbed this information with an expression of indifference, swallowing down the last drop of vodka, then saying: "No thanks. We're off too."

When they had pushed their way through the crowd to the pub door Judy said: "Oh dear. Sorry Leo. 'Fraid I've got to vanish again. Shan't be a sec. 'Bye Toby." She turned back into the crowd.

Toby Crest raised his eyebrows and shook his head with an amused expression, saying nothing. He opened the pub door and stretched out his hand. "We may all get a little damp I think. There's a few spots of rain. Still, not much. Quite pleasant really. And a firework display too at no extra charge.

Well, goodbye. Thanks again for the drink." He sauntered off to the left, hands in pockets. Selver watched him go, feeling frankly envious. That was how he wanted to be, young, happy-go-lucky and fancy-free.

Selver put on his jacket and stepped out into Gresse Street. Lightning forked across the sky above the Birkbeck College like a gigantic vivid vein. The thunder was louder now, which meant the storm must be moving towards central London. He turned his face up to the rain with a feeling of gratitude for the refreshing sensation. He started as a hand caressed the back of his neck. Judy said: "Sorry! You weren't expecting that. I really love lightning. It's so exciting!"

The fitful glare of the flashes was having a strange effect on colours, making Judy's eyes appear like the translucent green of grapes. She took Selver's hand and put it round her waist, saying: "It's just a short dash home. Hold on now—I'm a little bit sloshed."

Just running along the wet streets, practically skidding round the corner, had a magically re-vitalising effect on Selver. When they reached the only house left standing on one side of Stephen Street past the large block known as Gresse Buildings, he found that his headache had vanished. Standing on the stone steps close to Judy as she opened her white purse he was excited by the feel of her warm bare flesh under his hand and the beginning curve of her breast. She turned to look at him with a strange, serious expression as if she was searching in his eyes for something. Her vivacity had deserted her. Their moods seemed to be linked by some strange see-saw apparatus. Now that she was not excited and provocative, Leo found himself in a state of sexual arousal.

"Handsome young chap, your friend Crest."

"Oh, he looks all right. But it's like talking to nothing. I mean, all the time you're chatting away he's thinking about Toby Crest. I prefer a bit of give-and-take myself." Judy opened the front door and switched on a feeble light to show a small hallway with torn brown lino on the floor and sombrely papered walls. She said: "Don't look at any of this. Straight in here."

She went through the first door on the right and fiddled with a bedside lamp. When it was lit a rather cosy-looking bedroom was disclosed, with a cream and gold colour scheme. There was a cream-coloured double bed, a cream and gilt wardrobe and a small dressing-table and stool. The room was bare of ornaments and photographs.

"Give me your jacket, darling. I keep on confiscating it, don't I? But you won't need it here."

Selver took off his jacket and Judy folded it neatly, putting it on the stool by the dressing-table. She moved towards the window. "Come over here. I want to watch the lightning." As he obeyed this order Selver realised that not only had his desire for her come back, but he was under her spell, going through the strange business that was always repeated when he fell for a woman, feeling like a youth again.

Standing by the silent girl looking into the street, Selver could see an odd fence in front of the demolished houses— it was made up of dozens of old doors nailed together in a row. This surrealistic image, illuminated by the on-and-off flicker of lightning, was like a scene in a nightmare: for just a moment Leo Selver stood paralysed by some strange, undefined fear.

The feeling left him as Judy pulled the curtains to with one hand and beckoned him with the other. She left one gap at the window through which she still stared out at the stormy sky. When he came to her side she turned immediately to kiss him. She threw her arms round his neck, holding him tightly, but her kiss was much less bold than the one with which their evening had commenced. Her mouth was closed and only yielded slightly at Leo's insistence. It banished the memory of the other over-sweet kiss. Leo moved his hands slowly up and down the girl's warm back beneath her jersey, slowly tracing every curve, lingering on the dimple-like depressions just above her trousers as if he was a blind man

47

committing her body to memory. Judy stood still, saying nothing, breathing deeply. His hands trembled as he undid her brassière, then commenced the slow rhythmical stroking again. He was high on the heady stuff of desire: the strange evening with the girl, the storm, the night to come, were all as magical and uncertain as life itself.

Judy pulled the curtain across the remaining gap. With a quick movement she tugged the brief jersey up over her head. Leo bent forward to kiss the tender skin below her armpit. Judy threw the jersey away and then pulled Leo's face on to her breasts.

VII

X STRODE along the dark London side-streets at midnight with a measured pace that did not alter, as though he were a clockwork model. His white-cotton-gloved hands were plunged deep in his white macintosh pockets. In his left hand he held a brass candlestick which had to be further concealed by the macintosh sleeve; in the other pocket there were a Yale key, a Guy Fawkes' mask of silver-coloured papier mâché, and a facsimile RM 109 Chief Special, an authentic model of one of his favourite revolvers, compact with a small grip and a two-inch barrel but of .38 calibre.

Walking with his head down, apparently plunged in thought, X was in fact intensely aware of his surroundings. Turning into Stephen Street, he raised his head for a searching look a few moments before reaching the steps to No. 14. The street was empty and he ran lightly up the steps, looking about him once more before using the Yale key to open the door. Once inside he stood still for a few moments, straining to catch any sounds in the house, then scrupulously wiped his feet on the mat. He put on the silver mask, pocketed the key, then took out the Chief Special and held it in his right hand. He held the candlestick in his left. Slowly he opened the first door in the hall. The dark room smelt of garlic. He stood still again, checking that the curtains were pulled across the windows, then bent down to turn on the bedside lamp. The light revealed the room to be in some confusion, with underclothes, a blanket and a gold-coloured quilt mixed up in a pile on the floor and a pair of white trousers precariously over the mirror on the dressing-table. Selver and the Latimer girl were sleeping entwined, covered only by a single sheet. They woke together and both struggled up with puzzled exclamations.

X pointed the small revolver at them while calmly surveying the room. He noticed a small gap in the curtains and backed over to put them in place.

The girl exclaimed: "God! What's that? What are you doing? You ..." Her expression became terrified as she noticed the candlestick. "You took that from here. Why's that? What are you going to do?"

Selver tried to say something in a high panicky voice but the excited words came out jumbled and drowned in a bubbling sound as if liquid was flooding his throat. He slid out of bed and stood up, clenching his fists. X's eyes glittered darkly and he moved his head slowly from side to side, conveying amusement at the puny threat.

Tugging the sheet off the bed the girl got up too; she held it in front of her as she stared at the candlestick, regarding it as an awesome object, even more frightening than the .38 revolver.

X said quietly: "Shtand shtill both of you. Don't move." He took two steps towards the girl, who called out: "Oh God! What do you really want? You said ..." in a voice that faltered and failed. Her lips trembled and her eyes were wide with terror. She stood in a hunched position, shaking uncontrollably, with both hands holding the sheet up to her mouth as though it might protect her. As X approached her she called out: "Oh no! God no! Please don't! You said ... Oh

49

please no!" Then she dropped the sheet and covered her face with her hands.

X struck the girl with the candlestick while keeping Selver covered with the gun. The savage blow was aimed at her head but her flinching movement made it strike her on the neck. She shed some blood in flying gobbets, floating streamers that shone lingeringly in the air like spittle dropping into a dentist's bowl. The second blow was just as hard and more accurate, hitting the back of her head with a sickening thud, sending her straight to the floor, twisted up with the sheet.

Selver had a bewildered expression; his mouth did not open but his throat kept working, as if he was continually swallowing. With a great effort, as though tackling a foreign language, he managed to get out some words. They were stretched out with dashes like conversation in a toddler's comic: "Bast-ard. Ab-so-lute bast-ard." For a moment Selver looked as if he might burst into tears, then he ran round the bed, his fists flailing. X hit him with the hand that held the revolver—a carefully judged blow, dismissive but not hard enough to do real damage. Selver fell down at the end of the bed, tried to get up immediately by pulling on the stool in front of the dressing-table and turned it over.

X crouched down on his haunches by the girl and did nothing for a few moments but breathe deeply. A little blood was still trickling from the wound in her neck. X dropped the candlestick on to the sheet. He looked over towards Selver, raising his left forefinger in front of his mouth aperture to indicate that Selver should remain quiet, but saw that the admonition had been superfluous. Selver looked partly stunned, and was having difficulty in breathing and making strange gasping noises.

Judy Latimer's eyes were glassily concentrated yet unfocused and unseeing. There was a good deal of blood on the sheet beneath her. X first held her unresisting wrist and then, after a movement of reluctance, put his gloved hand on her heart. He concentrated his attention on the girl's corpse for a minute before turning to Selver and saying: "Now we're going to have a little chat. Do you understand? Just a few words but they'd better make sense. You'll tell me the truth. Everything I want to know. Otherwise ..." He pointed with the Chief Special first at the girl and then at Selver.

Selver was still on his knees at the end of the bed, gasping, with the palms of both hands flat on the carpet, apparently trying to get to his feet but unable to make it. Veins stood out in his puckered forehead though the lower part of his face was ashen and blank. He uttered a low moaning noise and opened his mouth wide as if going to scream, but no sound came. He made an odd movement like that of a badly deformed man with arms so small as to be useless, suddenly falling in an unprotected way. His jaw snapped shut as his chin hit the carpet. The pale skin of his face began to blotch with red. The fingers of his right hand moved feebly on the carpet, stroking the pile. He made a convulsive grabbing movement as if to get his balance, then lay still. His head was twisted at an unnatural angle and his tongue lolled out of the side of his mouth.

X pocketed the Chief Special and moved quickly towards Selver, saying vehemently "Oh shit", tugging him up and supporting his head. X's eyes moved wildly behind the mask. He took a pillow from the bed and put it under Selver's head, then felt his pulse and began to massage his heart. The red flush had completely died away from Selver's face leaving it as white as flour. His body was cold. After a few minutes of massaging X stopped and picked up a small mirror from the dressing-table, placing it in front of Selver's slack mouth. X quietly said a string of obscenities when he saw there was no sign of breathing.

Repeating the word "Shit" over and over again, X got up from the floor and picked up Selver's jacket and trousers. He went through each pocket, carefully replacing some pound notes, a cheque-book, credit cards and a driving-licence. There were several scraps of paper in one jacket pocket and he took

51

all of them. Then he dragged Selver's body over to the girl's and pushed Selver's left hand into the blood-stained sheet, and folded the cold fingers of his right hand firmly round the candlestick.

Taking off the silver mask, X went and stood at the side of the room so that he could examine it carefully. He took some time over this, stooping once to replace the mirror on the dressing-table. He checked the contents of his pockets, making sure that he had the Yale key, the revolver and the mask, then went out of the room leaving the bedside lamp lit.

VIII

TURNING the two hand-mirrors this way and that did not improve matters. At each different angle Beatrice Selver found that she was confronted by a depressing image of slack neck muscles and a double chin. There was a puffy look about her eyes and her skin was dry. From unexpected encounters with her image reflected in shop windows Beatrice knew that she was in the habit of tightening up her face muscles before studying herself in a mirror, but now even that piece of self-deception did not stop her from being confronted with the unpleasing picture of a fat lined face. It was not surprising that Leo wanted someone younger and more attractive. It was unfair that men so often kept their looks better than women as they got older.

Beatrice sighed, put down the mirrors, walked over to the hand-basin and splashed her face with cold water. Lying down during the day was a mistake and she blamed the puffiness partly on her nap, but after walking the entire length of the Marine Parade to Roedean and missing lunch she had felt unusually tired. No, weary was the only word to describe her sensation on returning to the small bedroom. It had been a stupid mistake to make a nostalgic anniversary trip to Brighton; to make it alone was an act of masochism and self-pity, mixed up with a sense of curiosity about how she would react to it. She had a different room from the one she had shared with Leo in August, 1953, and the place had been altered slightly, but even entering the front door to the West Hotel in Oriental Place had subjected her to all sorts of odd memories and emotions. It had been a funny sort of holiday then, with so little money to spend, and Leo off much of the time visiting all the antique shops in The Lanes, and Dave Buchanan spending each morning playing bowls; but she and Edna Buchanan had been happy just sitting on the beach talking while the little boys played or watching them sail boats in the pool near the putting-green.

Standing at the window, craning her head in order to see the end of the West Pier, Beatrice remembered Leo's joky reaction when they had been shown to their poky room at the back of the hotel in 1953; how he had stood on a chair and used his hands as pretend binoculars in order to obtain the advertised "sea view". He had been a different person then, happy and content, always joking or singing. She remembered one evening after they had come back from a show on the pier he had produced a bottle of sparkling white wine and two glasses borrowed from the dining-room and they had gone down to sit on the beach by the Palace Pier in the moonlight, and he had sung "Isn't it romantic?". Another evening it had rained and they had stayed in their room taking their turn to "baby-sit" while Edna and Dave Buchanan had gone off to the pictures, and Leo produced a pack of cards and quoted some lines from a poem she had not heard previously:

> Cupid and my Campaspe playd
> At cards for kisses; Cupid payd:
> He stakes his quiver, bow and arrows ...

Beatrice Selver shook her head as if that physical act would help in shaking off pleasant memories that had turned sour.

She put on her lilac-coloured cotton frock and the matching sandals, flicked her short black hair with a comb, made up her lips, and left the room and memories of happier bygone years.

Descending the narrow stairs she felt remote and detached from all that was happening in the streets and on the beaches of Brighton; she did not feel at all as if she was on holiday, but like an observer sent to spy on life, picking up odd snatches of conversation, mentally snapping the tall old man in the hall who was sucking his teeth and staring morosely at the poster which showed the entertainments available in the town.

There was no one at the small reception-desk and she put down her room key, obsessed with what a queer, solitary business life was. Everyone was always alone and only made contact with others to a certain extent, so that you could spend a quarter of a century living with someone and yet not know what was really going on in his head.

Walking down Oriental Place to King's Road, she could see that the dark clouds which had brought the shower at lunch-time were being blown away to the south-east towards France. Some raindrops were still poised on the windscreens of cars, in perfect half-balls, but the pavements were practically dry. Lots of young families were making for the beach. For a moment Beatrice felt lost and indecisive, on the edge of tears; then a stout man went past her, belching discreetly, and she felt saved by that common touch of humanity. Her mood of depression was probably due partly to feeling empty: she had eaten only one small piece of toast for breakfast. The unimaginative menus at the West Hotel made it relatively easy to keep on a diet. Suddenly she remembered that twenty years before there had been a large goldfish bowl in the hotel dining-room and Leo had often pretended to shake pepper and salt over the bowl, much to the amusement and consternation of Eddy Buchanan and little Billy respectively.

Beatrice Selver stood at the edge of the promenade just in

front of the empty bandstand: the tide was in and there seemed to be an expression on the face of the gently lapping sea, one of peace and contentment such as she now only experienced occasionally in dreams. She hated growing old but Leo's behaviour made the experience worse than it need be: if only they could share everything together. Instead he seemed to be getting continually more secretive. No doubt he was having another affair but she was no longer anxious to know what was going on in that way: she did not try to catch him out in lies as she had done. But now there was an additional area of secrecy, all this intimacy and curious feigned friendship with Sidney Chard, a man whom Leo used to criticise bitterly. She had often puzzled her brains over his new relationship with Chard but she could not understand it.

She looked over at the Hotel Metropole with a fleeting ironic memory of how very grand it had seemed to her in 1953. She sniffed the sea air appreciatively; she admitted to herself that she was hungry and was going to depart from her regimen of no lunch to the extent of just one sandwich and a cup of coffee. There was a small café in Air Street, up by the Clock Tower, where they served delicious simple sandwiches made with wholemeal bread. At first she thought she would stick to classic cucumber, but the idea of one containing crabmeat, lettuce and mayonnaise became more and more enticing, with a *cappuccino*, and perhaps one slice of cake.

Beatrice's step became quicker as she walked up West Street. The idea of this trip had fascinated her, but now she could admit that it had been a mistake: she would cut it short and go home. Having decided this she felt as though a weight had been removed from her. She laughed at the absurdity of her position in practically regarding this holiday as a short term of imprisonment. The cats would be delighted to see her return. There was a lot to do in the garden. She had made up her mind that next year she would have the bed nearest to the cottage full of old-fashioned scented flowers:

55

stocks, mignonette, alyssum, tobacco plants, lilies. Her mind became full of plans for changing her life, doing all the decorating she had put off for so long, undertaking more voluntary work in the village. One thing she was quite definite about now: never to make another nostalgic expedition into the past.

As Beatrice Selver crossed the traffic from West Street going towards the café in Air Street, she felt more positive and optimistic than she had done for some months. She thought that perhaps the few days by the sea had done her some good after all. Going past the Clock Tower towards the café her mind just registered a sensational newspaper placard:

SEX MURDER OF QUIET GIRL
Two Dead in Condemned House Horror

IX

AFTER five months in the Greek Islands when Ed Buchanan returned to London his total loot amounted to three hundred drachma notes, a silver coin, skin practically blackened by working long hours in the sun, stringy bleached hair, a pack of cards he had bought at a tobacco kiosk in Athens and a vicious-looking German cut-throat razor.

The ivory-handled razor, together with an enormous loaf, a jar of fresh olives and a bottle of sickly sweet banana cordial, had been given to him as a reward for pulling a drowning child out of the sea at Konstantinos. The razor had probably been one of the most valued possessions of the small boy's peasant father and Buchanan had accepted it only after it had been pressed on him persistently; now he had added it to the handful of things he intended to hang on to in his travels.

Shaving with the cut-throat was a pleasant experience, a

less finicky business than with an ordinary razor and much more efficient. He could have done with it during his first week on Santorini when he had got sunburnt rather badly. He finished off the shave with a flick under the chin, then washed his face and the razor. After drying the ivory handle with a towel he used a tissue on the blade. It was difficult to estimate the age of such a piece of craftsmanship. The motto *"Gott mit uns"* had been neatly carved on the handle, but that was obviously the work of one of its owners; the maker's name "Ebner" and the place "München" were engraved in tiny letters on the blade.

Buchanan considered the razor an interesting relic and thought it probable that it had a dramatic history. It had been given to him during a long *retsina* session, with olives and various fried titbits, while his clothes were being dried in the peasant's tiny cottage. Buchanan's Greek was fragmentary but he had understood the boy's father to say it had once belonged to a German soldier, the statement being accompanied by a throat-slitting gesture. He could not remember at what stage in the Second World War Greece had been invaded or whether the German occupation had extended to all the islands, including those like Samos, which was within sight of the Turkish mainland. There had been a fascinating faded photograph on the wall of the cottage showing a group of soldiers in a motley of uniforms. For the hundredth time he had wished that his Greek had been good enough to ask a few questions.

Buchanan opened a door in the luxurious bathroom and was confronted by the biggest airing-cupboard he had ever seen, containing a large collection of sheets and blankets and piles of freshly laundered shirts. Buchanan owned three denim shirts that needed washing and one made of checked cotton which was practically worn out but clean. He pulled it on, and the dark blue trousers and heavy brown boots he had bought in a tiny shop at Karlovasi on the island of Samos.

The flight back from Athens to London had been bang

on time and it had been nice to arrive early enough to collect his mail and do a little shopping for basic provisions. He walked into the splendid large kitchen that opened on to a balcony facing east with an oblique view of the Thames up to Chelsea Bridge. He put on a kettle to make some instant coffee and opened the larder. There were brown paper bags containing tomatoes, bananas, mushrooms and figs, with a malt loaf that looked soggy with goodness. Two bottles of milk and a packet of Normandy butter in the fridge had completed his purchases. It had been some time since he had had to provide his own meals but he did not think he had made any mistakes.

Standing in the sun on the balcony, nibbling a banana and drinking coffee, Buchanan was aware of how good it was to be alive, and was grateful for his blessings. He knew that he had never been fitter in his life. He could heartily recommend four months of hard labour in the sun, with plenty of swimming and a simple diet planned by a Californian hippy health food fanatic. It was on Samos that Buchanan had come his closest to prayer, on one of his rare days off from building a guest-house and *taverna*, accompanying his young bosses Stella and Niko Messisklis on a picnic. After the midday snack of *paximadia* and goat's cheese with some *tsikoudia*, a *raki* flavoured with mulberries, he had left the young married couple to enjoy their siesta and walked off in the direction of a remote mountain village. The area to the east of Karlovasi was one of the most beautiful he had seen, pattened with streams and lush meadows, dotted with cypresses, olive groves and vallonia oaks. There was a handful of white-washed cottages with great pitchers and ribbed *amphorae* standing by the doorways, and he had seen one small white chapel made splendid with blue and gold paint. The sights all around him, the delicious scents of herbs and flowers, the warmth of the sun, had seemed so good that at one point he had felt like throwing himself on the ground with some vague prayer of thanks to whatever gods might be.

The sound of a phone summoned Buchanan back from his idyllic memories. He picked up the white receiver in the kitchen with a wary approach. A young woman said: "This is Bathwick Mews Performance Cars. Can I speak to Mr. Buchanan?"

"Buchanan speaking."

"Oh, good, will you hold on please. Mr. Hughes calling."

"Ed, is that you?"

"Yes, Ken. How are you mate? Thriving as usual?"

"Just fair, Ed, fair. Moving along. How come? I mean how about this posh Chelsea address. Swan Walk? Did you rob a Greek bank?"

"Much easier than that. No sweat at all. A bloke I met at the last address I sent you, at the Kalamaki Beach Hotel, he offered to lend me this place rent-free for up to a month, I was just having a chat with him and a couple of girls over drinks, and *voilà*."

"What's the catch?"

"Beats me. Nothing I can see so far. This guy said that with the robbery rate round here being what it is he preferred to have someone sleeping in the place. He's got a lot of expensive junk, statues, that kind of thing. Truth is, now I see the place I think this chap, this Philip Tureck, well maybe he's a little AC-DC."

Ken Hughes laughed. "Well, you're away then, deary. You don't have to do any little chores, like take the peke out for walkies, that kind of thing?"

"Funny you should say that. Tureck did mention a cat called Jake, but I got the impression it was a ginger tom who just looked in for the odd meal on the balcony."

"That doesn't sound too arduous. Well, tell me, how do these gay surroundings suit you?"

"They don't worry me. Fact is, I could get used to all this luxury. I must say though, I didn't get a gay impression of Tureck at Kalamaki. He fooled me by making such a strong play for a blonde *fräulein* I rather fancied myself. But this

59

place! There's a fountain in the hall with a bronze statue that pees into it at the drop of a switch. It's the only time I've ever slept in lavender linen sheets. The bathroom's pale green with matching towels. And if he lives to be a hundred Tureck's never going to run out of bath salts and after-shave."

"Sounds like, play your cards right, you'll never want for anything again. But, seriously, how would the offer of a job appeal at the moment?"

"What job?"

"Same old job here, but better prospects."

"How's that?"

"Fact is, I'm getting tired of all this hacking about. If you shaped up perhaps you could take over from me in a year or so."

"That's a nice offer, Ken. Thanks. I'll give it serious thought. The thing is, you see, I enjoyed what I was doing in Samos so much I rather hanker after finding something else like that. Not that there's much chance."

"What exactly were you doing there? Your cards were very vague."

"First off I visited five islands in two weeks, just bumming around. Then I happened to meet this nice young couple in their early twenties, Stella and Nick. She's a hippy-type refugee from California who craves the simple life. He's a Greek, born in Samos. They're building a little guest-house and *taverna* right on the beach a couple of miles west of Karlovasi. A beautiful spot where a small river flows down the mountain. Their site is bang on the river where there was a fisherman's cottage. For four months I helped them, nine hours a day, a real slog. I turned up hundreds of barrowloads of cement by hand. Funny thing was, I've never been happier."

"You lived with them?"

"Yes."

"Just you and a couple of kids. Didn't you feel at all *de trop* at times? Is that what happened finally?"

60

"No. What happened was they ran out of money. So they had to stop temporarily. He's working in a leather-tanning factory. She's taken a job in the town. Next year, with what they save, they'll finish the place. Wish I could be there, but I don't know. My plans are vague at the moment. But I'll be in one day, Ken, and we'll have a chat. Don't think I'm not grateful."

"Okay, old lad. No rush. Just give me a ring and we'll have lunch. By the way, do you owe any money? We've had some punters in here inquiring about you."

"That's funny. Some income tax perhaps. Did you get their names?"

"Well, one said he was a friend of yours. Leo Selver. You know him? Nice bloke I thought."

"Oh yes, I know Leo. He was my father's friend really, but I've known him all my life. Did he leave a message?"

"No, just said he'd call again. I've been away on holiday myself since then, a humble kiddies' bucket-and-spade job in Brittany, so I'm a bit vague about whether he has in fact called again. But another bloke called twice, a funny-looking chappy with glasses. He was very persistent about contacting you, and finally that young fool Alec Finzi showed him your postcard with the Hotel Kalamaki address. I was annoyed about that. Didn't want you to have any follow-ups."

"No need to worry about that, Ken. I'm very grateful to you for letting me use your address and keeping those letters for me."

"Yes, you had quite a pile. You seem to be much in demand. Tell me, how is it no one offers me the loan of a luxurious flat?"

"It's all these capped teeth I've got. They have a hypnotising effect after a bit. Well, thanks again about the mail. Haven't read any of it yet. Perhaps my premium bonds have come up."

"Cheers then, Ed. Remember about the job. Could use you

61

here. But the wages won't pay for a Swan Walk flat and a cat called Jake."

"It's tough on Jake but I shall be out of here the moment I find a cheap room. See you."

Buchanan replaced the phone, puzzled by the news of the "funny-looking chappy with glasses" and Leo Selver. The last time he had seen Leo had been at his parents' funeral and then he had got a rather sour impression of him, of someone world-weary and cynical, standing around outside the crematorium at a loss for anything to say, with an expression of suppressed boredom; whereas good old Bee had found it so easy and natural to convey her sympathy. He could not imagine that Leo would take the trouble of going to Bathwick Mews just in order to seek advice about what new car he should buy.

Buchanan buttered a chunk of malt bread and sliced up the remains of the banana on it, then made some more coffee. He had a leisurely programme for the day that consisted of buying a couple of new shirts and possibly a pair of trousers and some kind of jacket. Then he must inquire about a paper that listed jobs in the country. Ken Hughes' offer was a good one but Buchanan hated the thought of going back into car-dealing, hacking about all over the country buying used sports cars. The world of car-dealing and the period when he had been a racing-driver now seemed equally remote and alien. Yet he could remember a time when driving a Formula One car, changing gears a thousand times in a race, with the excitement of surviving among the familiar stench of hot tarmac and high-octane fuel, had seemed uniquely absorbing. It was during his racing career that he had come across a comment from a high-wire artiste: "To be on the wire is life and the rest is waiting", and then he had agreed about the excitement of backing your life on your own skill. Now he wanted something more positive and creative, no matter on how small a scale. Ideally he wanted the chance to build up a place as they had done in Karlovasi, perhaps a derelict farm, though he could not imagine the opportunity occurring in Britain. It was the pioneering aspect that particularly appealed to him, the struggle to improvise and do things with inadequate equipment, preferably with a girl who fancied the same kind of life. But if it came off, what would happen once the derelict place was brought into use? He could not see himself in the role of a farmer.

He took out the silver coin that Stella Messisklis had given him as a good-luck piece when they said goodbye: his desire for possessions was very slight but he liked the worn old coin showing the little owl of Pallas Athene, its body in profile and its head full face. He could not imagine being happier than he had been when he and Nick were practically overwhelmed with the tasks they had to tackle in temporarily damming the river and putting in foundations for the terrace on the river bank; a long swim when work was done and returning to the smell of fried onions, and finding Stella slicing tomatoes, garlic and green paprika pods: then after dinner the sessions of drinking *ouzo*, playing cards and puzzling over Greek letters, the triple loop of Xi, the bisected almond of Theta, while Nick confused matters by turning P's into R's, B's into V's and the H's into E's.

Taking his plate and beaker to the sink, Buchanan sighed. He had found the good life for a while and now it was gone. There was no doubt that he missed it badly, with a peculiar sensation like homesickness. He turned on the water-heater and then fetched the greengrocer's carrier-bag which contained all his mail forwarded to the Bathwick Mews address. He emptied the bag on the kitchen table and spread the contents out like a pack of cards, looking for anything that appeared interesting. Nearly all of them were typed and there were a lot of official-looking manilla envelopes, with a good proportion of throw-away circulars. He opened one blue envelope, addressed in a childish hand, which had been forwarded to three different addresses. It contained a request for his autograph from a boy in Birmingham. Buchanan was amused to think how little value his signature must now command, even as swop material. Perhaps the lad was set on obtaining signatures of all the surviving drivers who had taken part in a particular race.

The white telephone rang again, and again Buchanan approached it warily. He had no prejudice at all about homosexuals and he could not remember meeting an unpleasant one, but he felt a little uncomfortable about appearing to be Philip Tureck's flat-mate.

There was the sound of a bronchial-type cough, some throat-clearing, and then a fussy voice inquired:

"Is that Mr. Edmund Buchanan?"

"It is."

"Ah good. Yes. Very good. How I hate dialling all those terrible digits! Oh for the good old days when one simply commanded the operator to summon up Flaxman or Gerrard or whatever."

It was a quavery, querulous old voice, the kind that seems to be full of a lifetime's irritations and frustrations, liable to become peevish given any provocation. Buchanan was curious as to what the old man could be going to say but did not try to hurry him and waited silently.

"Well then, my dear sir. This is Mr. Quentin speaking. Mr. Quentin of Loving Care."

"Loving what?"

"Loving Care, laddie. The cattery. Our motto, d'you see, really loving care! Mr. Philip Tureck sent me a card saying you were *in situ* and would probably be willing to look after Jake at home. I'm afraid Jake's been pining a bit."

"So you've got the cat. Funny, Tureck did mention a cat but I got the impression it was just a stray who occasionally looked in here for a meal."

"Don't be whimsical, dear boy. Jake a stray! Jake is a beautiful big ginger male. Very much a home-loving and luxury-craving creature. So you can call and pick him up the tooter the sweeter? Here I mean."

Buchanan brooded for a moment. Having the cat would tie him to the flat for a while, but it seemed rather mean to refuse and it would be some kind of company. "All right. Where do I go? And how do I transport him?"

"Jake's luxurious, leather-handled basket is here, laddie. That's no problem."

"And here is?"

"Loving Care. 106B Rushcroft Road, top floor that is. Brixton. Do you know Brixton?"

"I do. Well, I used to. They can't have changed it all in five years."

"They haven't. Then you probably know Brixton's famous Market Row. Rushcroft Road is about a minute from the market."

"Near the stewed-eels caff?"

There was a pause and when Quentin spoke again a slight change in his tone had taken place, as if the facetious old man had been replaced by one equally quavery but more down to earth. "Quite right. You do know Brixton I see. Very good. Well then, Jake and I will be waiting for you. The cattery's in the yard at the back, but come straight up to 106B first. Goodbye." The phone went dead before Buchanan could say anything else.

X

LONDON seemed like a heightened version of itself to Ed Buchanan as he made his way to the Loving Care cattery in Brixton—the buses redder, the traffic noises louder, the streets busier, and the voices more cockney than he remembered. He was an authentic cockney himself, born in Hanbury Street well within the sound of Bow Bells, and his childhood had been spent largely in the East End; but living in a remote cottage on Samos for four months had affected him, so that he was irritated by the continuous flow of traffic racing along the Chelsea Embankment. Normally he prided himself on his knowledge of the metropolis, but when he got to Chelsea Bridge Road he felt for a moment like a country bumpkin puzzling about the quickest route to take him south of the river.

Walking along Buckingham Palace Road to Victoria Station, part of his mind was still engaged with the puzzle posed by Leo Selver calling in at Bathwick Mews. He had only one real aunt but as a child he had always addressed the Selvers as "Uncle Leo" and "Aunty Bee". For some years his brief seaside holidays had been spent in their company, and the families' mutual Christmas festivities had been largely organised by Leo, who liked devising games such as the elaborate annual treasure-hunt which had taken them into each room in the adjoining houses.

Memories of Leo: driving his battered old Austin Seven in a car park while sitting on the floor so that it appeared to be without a driver; fooling about at beach cricket by pretending to run for a catch then falling down into the sea; his transparent card-tricks, and the card houses built with trembling hands; his repertoire of 1930s songs which he would sing mimicking Bing Crosby's voice. Looking back Buchanan realised that he had spent more of his time during those early seaside holidays with Leo than with his father—Leo had always seemed to really enjoy digging large sand-castles with a system of moats, canals and walls to keep out the returning tide, fishing in rock-pools and playing clock-golf. All that had been changed by Billy Selver's death: within a few months the Selvers had moved to Hendon, the first of a series of moves, each one of which had taken them further away and decreased the opportunities of family meetings. Buchanan decided that he must look Leo up as soon as possible—it seemed likely that there had been an important reason for his calling in at Bathwick Mews.

The train slowed down just after crossing the Thames and juddered to a halt by Battersea Power Station. Buchanan looked down river towards Vauxhall Bridge and surveyed the desolate Nine Elms Lane area where rows of tiny houses were grouped round the gas-works, goods depots and railway-sidings. He missed the idyllic Samos beach setting where he had worked against a background noise of waves endlessly breaking, with the sea's salt smell mixed up with rosemary and myrtle under a cloudless blue sky, but London still had a fascination which would take him down any street he did not know.

As the train started again Buchanan was wondering how much Brixton had changed in the five years since he had been there—he had read the odd, disturbing story about trouble between the local people and immigrant West Indians but he could not believe it was being transformed into a ghetto area of the kind which bred bitterness and undirected hatred. He had vivid and unpleasant memories of two such areas abroad: one called Hunters Point south of San Francisco and the other named the Quartier de la Porte d'Aix, the part of Marseilles known as the "Kasbah". He could still visualise the straight and narrow streets of the "Kasbah", with washing hung out from all the windows of the tall buildings and the walls held up by vast timber buttresses; the rows of bright tinsel dresses for the Berber ladies, and Chinese indigo cotton smocks; the Algerian ladies trying not to be noticed and the Kabyles with tattooed faces; the rue de Chapeliers thronged with street vendors and bargaining shoppers. Buchanan's broken nose was a memento of the "Kasbah", the result of tangling with three Senegalese dandies who had been beating up a member of the Deuxième Corps Cycliste outside Black's Paradise Bar.

Ed Buchanan had inherited his father's height, large-boned build and exceptional strength. In his early twenties he had been a finalist in the A.B.A. light-heavyweight class and for a short period he had worked as a bouncer in a Nice nightclub so he was not particularly perturbed at the prospect of being mugged in Brixton, but he disliked the idea of any part of London becoming dangerous in that way. He also liked many of the qualities that the West Indians had—it was only a few years since he had been a habitué of a Jamaican restaurant and occasionally attended shebeens in Brixton's Somerleyton Road. From what he knew of the tough south Londoners he would have thought they were the ideal community to absorb the coloured people who wanted to live there.

Leaving the railway station Buchanan bought a newspaper and mentally framed the advertisement he wanted to find in its columns: "Energetic self-reliant man required to put a derelict farm in good order. The farm is situated on an estuary and the farmhouse and seawall will have to be rebuilt. Successful applicant to be working partner ...'

The pleasant daydream faded as Buchanan walked along the busy Atlantic Road and turned into the street-market that ran down Electric Avenue. The atmosphere was just like that of the markets in Berwick Street or Portobello Road, noisy and jolly, with lots of cockney banter as passers-by were tempted with bargains. A few of the stalls were run by West Indians and there was a high proportion of coloured shoppers, but the air of gaiety could not have been less like the sullen brooding atmosphere of Hunters Point.

An amplifier in one of the shops was blasting out the reggae song "Wonderful World" in which the West Indian viewpoint was proclaimed through the voice of Jimmy Cliff:

> Under the sun, moon and stars
> Got to have some fun
> Before my life is done ...

Buchanan had been a fan of reggae since its early days when it was known as rocksteady, bluebeat and ska. He liked the heavy drum-beat rhythms with, at their roots, the music of "sufferation", of the miserable shanty-town life of rural migrants to Jamaica's capital of Kingston, and the strange cults like the Rastafarians with their home-made drums and rumba-boxes.

There were some coloured teenagers in floppy velvet caps and knitted tea-cosies walking through the market, a group of coloured children with great big eyes and wonderful smiles, and a couple of Rastafarians whose thick matted tassels of hair hung down over their shoulders, greeting each other with "Wha' happen man?", the West Indian hello. But they all seemed to fit into the market with its cockney atmosphere of live-and-let-live. Buchanan felt very much at home there and within a few minutes he had bought a carrier, some pink-fleshed grapefruit, sweet potatoes and a cheap cheesecloth shirt. Walking through Market Row he could not resist a bottle of Captain Bligh rum from St. Vincent even though it meant he would be rather encumbered when it came to dealing with Jake's "luxurious, leather-handled basket".

He grinned to himself at the memory of his one-sided conversation with the querulous Mr. Quentin. He was looking forward to meeting both Quentin and Jake. There was an odd building on the corner of Rushcroft Road, with glossy green tiles among the brickwork and stained-glass windows, that looked as if it must have been a cross between a church and municipal baths before being converted into flats and shops. Rushcroft Road had a depressed, deserted air; some of the houses were shabby, the biscuit-coloured bricks blackened by grime and the paintwork peeling.

The door of No. 106 was open. Quentin had said that he should come upstairs, so Buchanan stepped inside to find a hallway floored with dirty green linoleum, and two closed doors both of which bore identical signs of the HIGHLIFE CLUB and sketchy paintings of a setting sun. He drummed his knuckles on one of the doors just for fun but there was no sound of any highlife.

The stairway leading to the second floor was as uninviting as the hall, with a badly torn threadbare carpet on the stairs and a pale green wall decorated with graffiti. Buchanan read a sign saying "Children beat your mother while she's young" and an involved invitation to some sexual assignation as he walked up the stairs. There was a smell of urine and carbolic disinfectant. Somewhere in the house he heard the sound of a sluggishly flushing lavatory.

Buchanan found there were three doors off the landing and they were all locked. He knocked on each one without any response. There was no sign to point to which might be considered 106B or the Loving Care cattery. He muttered "Lots of luck" to himself. Had the call from the strange Mr. Quentin been some kind of involved joke—had he been sent to Rushcroft Road on a wild-goose chase? Remembering the sound of the flushing lavatory he banged on each door again, listening intently for any sound on the other side, and tried the handles in vain. After waiting for a few minutes more he reluctantly returned to the head of the stairs.

A heavily built man with wavy black hair that had no parting and was too good to be true stood in the hallway below with an unpleasant smirking expression. He looked Buchanan up and down and called out: "Buch'n. Yes, you, fuck-face. I want you."

Buchanan said nothing but gave the man a short, dangerous look.

The man in the black wig moved slowly towards the stairs. He had impassive flat features, but a scar that began by his mouth twisted it into a perpetual smirk. He was dressed in light grey trousers, a white shirt and a black cardigan. His eyes were dull and purposely vacant like those of an old man. Despite the blank eyes and the wig, Buchanan judged him to be in his late thirties or early forties. He had a massive chest, bulging biceps and the bullying air of a threatener, the kind who was paid to make late-night calls to scare tenants out of slum property.

Buchanan called down: "What's your problem?"

"Problem, shitbag? The problem is you've got these fucking

70

coons all of a mogador. I mean it's the bleeding aggro. You've been leanin' on 'em too hard so now I have to do sumfin, don't I?"

Buchanan was trying to think of some enemy from his past life who could possibly have arranged this little meeting for him. The bruiser knew his name, so it was not a chance encounter with a nut. He had thought the phone-call from Quentin was slightly odd, but he had been put off his guard because it had tied in with what Philip Tureck had told him about the cat at the Swan Walk flat. That meant that Tureck must also somehow be involved in this assignation, which seemed absurd. Buchanan called down to the wig man: "You've got me mixed up with somebody else."

The man's eyes had a practically reptilian slowness but now there was a flash of malice in them as he said: "Don't try to moody me. You're the fucker I want all right." He held out his clenched fists like weapons for inspection. "Yes, I'm goin' to hospitalise you—make you piss blood."

Somewhere deep inside his head Buchanan was smiling—a trait he would have to watch. When his release from the Police Force was being talked over, during the final interview that had led up to his resignation, a good deal had been made of the fact that he was too emotional to make a good copper; but underneath that he had the impression that they had diagnosed the interior aggression which he always had to keep controlled. With this bruiser he was going to make an exception: inner tensions could not find a better object if they had to be released. He dropped his carrier-bag, grinned, and said: "Well come on then", walking back a few steps.

The man in the wig stopped at the top of the stairs and indicated the narrowness of the passage, saying, "This is real neat. Stand still, you prick, you're not goin' anywhere." He gave a little puffy whimper of a laugh.

Buchanan stood with his legs spread wide apart—he had learnt in his first boxing lesson that to punch effectively you need a sound base. He held his fists high and watched the

71

man in the wig lumbering towards him, blocking the first sizzling punch and stepping inside the next one. His opponent was what Henry Cooper called "an arm puncher", someone who punches from the shoulder rather than with the shoulder behind the blow. Buchanan jabbed continually with his left, short but accurate punches that kept finding their target. The man in the wig had little science and was obviously used to beating down any opposition with a flurry of massive blows. Buchanan took some stick while waiting for an opening, including a very heavy punch to the chest. Another one seared his cheek, too close for comfort to his capped teeth. But that punch took the man in the wig a little off balance. Buchanan promptly brought his left knee up in the man's crotch and tapped his head back with two jolting left jabs. Then he brought his right across, a punch he felt was solid all the way, with thirteen stone weight behind it, the kind of punch his father used to call "Good night nurse".

As the man in the wig staggered back Buchanan used him like a punching-bag, hitting him with every combination he knew. The man's head banged against a doorway and Buchanan caught him on the rebound with a right uppercut to the point of his chin. A boxer never sees the punch that knocks him out. The man's eyes became vacant and he slithered down in the hallway. Buchanan said quietly: "You fell real neat", and crouched beside him.

The man in the wig moved his feet about in an aimless sort of way: the will was there for him to get up for another round, but willpower wasn't enough to do the trick. One heavy-veined hand scrabbled with the edge of his cardigan as if to find something inside. Buchanan said lightly: "Don't reach for anything apart from a sandwich because I'll make you eat it."

The man on the floor raised his head a little way up against the door to make his posture more comfortable, but tried no other movements.

Buchanan said: "Who sent you? Was it Quentin?"

The man in the lop-sided wig gingerly felt his chin, looked Buchanan straight in the eyes and grinned, showing yellow side teeth and bridge-work that did not match too well. The derisive grimace was meant to demonstrate to Buchanan that a lot more punishment would be needed before any information would be forthcoming. Buchanan's aggressive instinct only surfaced in retaliation and did not extend to hitting someone prone on the floor. He got up, collected his carrier-bag and ran down the grimy stairs. He thought there was a possibility that Quentin might have arranged more surprises for him and was glad to find that his exit from 106 Rushcroft Road was not barred.

XI

At 1 p.m. on Wednesday the 12th September 1973 Ed Buchanan was standing outside Leo Selver's antique shop in Crawford Street. It had taken him only an hour from the moment he had read Beatrice Selver's letter to reach the shop, and this included time spent in re-packing the things he had taken from his case in the Swan Walk flat. His decision to go immediately to Bee had been instinctive, and he had acted impulsively as he so often did. On looking into the window of the shop and seeing only a tall thin girl moving an oak chest about, he realised it was possible that Bee was not there but at her cottage in Hampshire. Now he stood holding a battered case, a duffle-bag and two carrier-bags containing all his worldly possession, feeling rather dubious as to what he should say to the girl. He put the case down and stared into the window while pondering the problem. His eye was taken, rather surprisingly as he had an antipathy to material possessions, by an elegant black leather harness with elaborate silver decorations including a coat of arms in three places. It was the only article in the shop window with an

73

explanatory note by it, in a neat small hand on a piece of white card. The language was so technical and specialised that he wondered who could have written it:

A SUPERB STATE CARRIAGE HARNESS in fine quality polished black leather: the hames, eyes, buckles, etc, all close silver plated, the drafts and trace ornaments with leafage and scroll-work, the terret surmounted by a marquess's coronet, the bearing rein pedestal, collar head-plate, quarter and girth straps all bearing the arms and supporters in close plate of the sixth Marquess Trewartha, of Trewartha Place, Cornwall. Arms: quarterly, 1st and 4th sa. on a fesse, between three lions' heads erased arg. as many mullets of the first.

"Eddy, Eddy!" Buchanan looked up from the notice on hearing this form of his name, used only by those who had known him as a child and by his ex-landlady in Wapping. Through the window he saw Beatrice Selver standing next to the tall slim girl and waving at him. He picked up his bags and moved round to the entrance of the shop, overwhelmed with feelings of depression and inadequacy. There were a few things he knew he could do well but a lot for which he was not equipped. He had no idea what to say to Bee about Leo's death. It would have been bad enough if Leo had simply died in an accident, but with the circumstances outlined in the newspaper cutting that had been enclosed in Bee's letter the problem was beyond him.

Once the glass door was opened and his bags were dumped on the floor, Beatrice made the sad meeting easier by silently putting out her arms towards him. It seemed natural to take her in his arms protectively and say nothing for a few moments. Memories of Bee spanning his lifetime flashed through his mind. He could remember evoking laughter when he was only three by stating his preference to sit on her lap in a crowded car, and as an adolescent her full figure and shapely legs had been the object of occasional lascivious thoughts; now he felt only protective fondness towards her. His warmth of feeling was due in part to memories of Leo as well as of her, for as a child they had acted like additional parents to him on occasions, and those were times he would never forget.

"Knew you'd come. If you could. Knew it ..." Beatrice spoke brokenly and Buchanan did not reply immediately. He was aware that she was on the verge of tears and did not want to provoke them by anything he said. "Of course, Bee." He pressed her shoulders. "I only got back from Greece yesterday afternoon and I collected my letters then, but I didn't start to open them till about an hour ago. I don't know what to say ..."

Beatrice Selver stepped back. Her face was pale but there was no sign of tears. "Katie!" She waved to the tall girl with carroty hair who had stood silently in the background. "Katie—this is Eddy Buchanan—you remember, I told you I had written to him. Katie Tollard's a friend and she's running the shop for me."

Katie Tollard smiled ruefully at Buchanan, saying: "*We* are running the shop—together." She had a thin face under the carroty hair, brown eyes and very white teeth. She was dressed in a dark brown cotton skirt and a short-sleeved cream shirt. She held out a thin strong hand to be shaken. "Hello."

"Hello." Buchanan pointed to his bags. "Sorry to clutter up the shop like this. I had the loan of a flat for last night but now I've left it—and I wanted to come straight here.'

Beatrice said: "Let's take them through to the back then. We were just going to have a cup of coffee. I'll make it while we talk."

Katie said: "I'll have mine later, Bee. You two talk. I must straighten up the mess I've made here and then phone Grantham about old Manny's Saddleworth jug. Okay? Just yell if you want me." She tugged at the oak chest again as she spoke. She had a brisk, business-like manner that matched her slim athletic figure and practical-looking hands.

75

Beatrice led the way from the large front room, sparsely decorated with pieces of antique furniture and several large clocks, into a smaller one at the back which was much more cluttered. This room had a slightly claustrophobic atmosphere for Buchanan who had definite ideas about the things he didn't want, which included the whole range of antiques; all the expensive junk in the world could be wheeled in front of him without evoking any interest.

There was a large desk in the small room. Beatrice slumped down in one of the two black leather armchairs beside it, sighed and shook her head. "Leo didn't kill that girl, Eddy. You know it's impossible—you know he couldn't have killed anyone. You remember what he was like. All the time I knew him I never saw him hit anyone. How could he have done it?"

"I know, Bee. It was an enormous shock—your letter and that cutting you sent. It seems incredible. That girl ..." Buchanan hesitated—if he were to say anything apart from just agreeing with Beatrice, if he were to make any intelligent contribution to the conversation, he was going to have to raise painful matters. "The girl Judy Latimer—did you know her?"

"No, I didn't—hadn't even heard her name. Of course he must have been having an affair with her. No doubt about that. But the fact that he had been sleeping with her doesn't mean he killed her. I can't bear that people should think that of Leo. What could have happened quite easily—though the police don't seem able to absorb this—is maybe she had some other man friend who found them together."

Buchanan nodded, feeling annoyed with himself for his inadequacy in this situation and also for the fact that his facility for critical observation continued to function even with dear old Bee in these tragic circumstances, noting that she had more lines round her mouth and eyes since he had last seen her, and that a well-cut dark blue frock could not disguise her growing plumpness. His encounter with the thug at 106

Rushcroft Road had left him in a puzzled and perturbed state of mind—having the tragic news of Leo's death on top of the Mr. Quentin mystery seemed to have disorganised his thinking so that he could not say anything sensible, but still his mental note-taking of appearances continued automatically.

He was grateful when Katie Tollard came into the room, saying: "I'm sorry to interrupt, Bee. I'll make the coffee. Grantham was useless about Manny's jug. He wouldn't say yes and he wouldn't say no. I think he's frightened we may make a cup of tea out of the deal." She looked across at Buchanan, directly into his eyes. He felt that their brief exchange of glances had some mysterious significance, like a sympathetic signal between them much more important than a long exchange of words.

Buchanan waited till Katie had opened a door at the back of the room into a scullery and then asked Beatrice: "What happened at the inquest?"

"Adjourned till—oh, about two weeks from now."

"Six weeks? That means they didn't see it as being an open-and-shut case then. What have they said to you?"

"Hardly anything. Of course they asked a lot of questions. A Detective Chief Superintendent Lucas is in charge I think. I suppose it's natural that they wouldn't take much notice of what I said."

Buchanan had enough experience of detective work to know the kind of boot-faced response there would have been to Beatrice's protests that her husband was incapable of killing anybody.

Katie looked through the scullery door while pouring coffee from a jug and said: "Lucas doesn't seem to have done much since the first time we saw him. It's a Detective Inspector Machin..."

"Bumper!" Buchanan exclaimed.

"Do you know him?"

"Yes—if it's Detective Inspector Charles Machin—I certainly do. Bumper is just a nickname from his days of football fame. Great soccer player. Good-looking chap, about three inches shorter than me, brown curly hair, fresh complexion? Geordie accent?"

"That's him. Not much of an accent but I thought he was north country."

"Yes, he's a Geordie." Before meeting Bumper Machin Buchanan had known hardly anything about the north-east of England, thinking of it just as the home of pigeon-racing, flat powerful ale and Andy Capp. Serving with Machin he had learnt a lot more and could still remember a snatch of a song Machin used to sing:

> Keep your feet still
> Geordie hinny.
> Let's be happy
>   through the neet.
> For we may not be
>   so happy through the day ...

This association of Buchanan and Machin seemed to have aroused Beatrice temporarily from her sad absorption in Leo's death. "When was this?" she asked. "Is he a friend of yours?"

"I haven't seen him for some time. But we were friends—well, it was a funny kind of relationship. We were good pals and then we both fell for the same girl. She chose Bumper—they got married—and I left the force. The first time that is —you remember, Bee—that was when I was a cadet."

"You were in the police yourself then?" Katie inquired as she entered carrying a tray with three gaily coloured mugs of coffee.

"Twice!" Buchanan said. "That's an admission of failure all right. My old man was in the Metropolitan force all his working life and had a reputation as a good copper and thief-taker. I joined as a cadet, left the force, then joined again some years later. I was allowed to do that mainly because of Pop's record. Then I left again—resigned, in fact, at the beginning of this year. I'm not cut out for the job. But

Bumper is. He's a belt-and-braces man. Very hardworking and efficient. He's not going to tell you what he's thinking but he's always thinking. You can rely on it."

"Would you see him for me, Eddy—could you do that?" Beatrice asked. "I've got some information—some odd facts that have puzzled us. He would probably take more notice if you talked to him. The strange thing is that I know Leo must have wanted to see you. He didn't keep a diary or a notebook, just wrote any notes and reminders down on scraps of paper. I found two notes about your address being care of the Bathwick Mews garage, and they must have been written recently because one was on the back of a card for the Bristol Antiques Fair that only took place in July."

"Yes, I know he wanted to see me. Ken Hughes, who owns the Bathwick set-up, told me that only this morning. He phoned to say that two men had called in and asked for me—and one of them was Leo."

"You see? There's no doubt in my mind that something was worrying him for weeks past, months in fact. I also found among his scraps of paper the card of a private-detective agency called Alpha Security—he'd scribbled down a time and date to call there so he must have actually talked to them. And another strange fact is that a friend of Leo's, a business friend called Sidney Chard—well it seems as if he left the country the very day Leo died. He went off in his car and hasn't been seen since."

"Nora, his wife, says that Sid went abroad," Katie volunteered. "But I know a girl who works for him. He's got an antique furniture shop in Camden Passage. This girl says she's quite sure that Sid hasn't gone abroad. Apparently he kept his passport in the office and it's still there."

"I've been thinking, Eddy"—Beatrice Selver spoke in a hesitant voice—"wondering if you might be willing to go to the Alpha Security people too and find out why Leo went there. I hate to bother you and don't know if you can spare the time, but it's the kind of thing I'm sure the police wouldn't

79

do. Would you? This private-detective business puzzles me so and I can't stop thinking about it."

"Of course, glad to do it. Time's no problem for me. At the moment I'm unemployed. Whether the Alpha people will talk to me is another matter. They're usually very strict about such things being confidential—they should be of course. But I'll go. Where is it?"

"Holborn I think. But I didn't mean now. I was also wondering—would you like to use our flat in Welbeck Street Mews? I shan't be staying there—Katie's putting me up while I'm working here, till I've decided what to do about the shop. So the Mews flat is empty and it seems a pity for you ..."

"That's a very kind offer, Bee—I accept, thank you. Frankly I hope it won't be for long—I want to find a job soon and live out of London—but meanwhile yes, thank you very much."

"One final offer," Katie added. "Have you had lunch? I know it sounds a funny time for it just after coffee but I missed mine, and as you said you came here in a rush I think you may have missed yours. Can you stand vegetarian food? There's a first-rate place just round the corner."

Buchanan got up smiling. He found it very easy to smile at Katie. "Sold!" he exclaimed. "I'm starving. What about you, Bee?"

Beatrice shook her head. "No, you two go. I had a sandwich and a Danish pastry at twelve I'm afraid."

XII

No sooner had they left the shop than Katie popped back into it again to pick up her purse. Buchanan gingerly probed one of his capped teeth with his tongue. The crown felt slightly loose and he mentally cursed whoever it was that had arranged for him to go to Brixton. He knew that his mild case of Francophobia stemmed not from the time he had been shot in the back by a French thug but the earlier occasion when he had been gypped over the crowns by a French dentist. With difficulty he stopped brooding on the possibility of more expensive dental work and finished reading the notice about the harness:

2nd. sa. a chevron between three spears' heads arg., the points embrued; 3rd. gu. an inescutcheon, vair between eight cross-crosslets or. Supporters: dexter, a griffin sa. beak and claws gu.; sinister, a lion rampant or, each gorged with a collar arg. charged with three mullets sa. Motto: FORTUNA FAVET AUDACI.

"Who wrote that note?" Buchanan asked Katie when she reappeared. He felt easy in her company, as if they had bypassed the preliminary getting to know each other and could talk about anything that came into their heads.

"Guilty. I wrote it, but with a lot of expert help. I did a good deal of that sort of thing for Leo. He had this fantastic flair, you see, that often wasn't backed up by knowledge. He would just *feel* something was really good of its kind, or valuable, or unique, and buy it. Then I did the research."

"Would that harness be valuable?"

"We think so. It's a fine example and in such marvellous nick, probably never used. Leo went to a sale in some remote part of Cornwall near Bodmin Moor, oh, about Easter time—I know it was held on an inconvenient date just before or after the holiday, and the weather was terrible, so hardly anybody turned up for the sale. Leo had a field-day there. The Trewartha family seems to have been an extremely odd bunch, turning out eccentrics every so often. The last marquess was a bachelor and a recluse for about thirty years—a very strange bloke indeed—groceries were left at the gates of the estate for him to collect, that sort of thing. Anyway he died last winter in a fire which gutted most of the house.

81

Firemen saved some of the things downstairs, in the hall and so on."

"Poor Bee. I still can't get over what a shock it must have been for her. I understood, reading the cutting, that Leo died of a heart attack. Is that right?"

"Yes. The police doctor reported 'a massive coronary occlusion'. Do you think that Bee is foolish to press for more inquiries?"

"I don't know. It's difficult for me—you see, I've known Leo all my life. My parents lived next door to the Selvers and they made rather a fuss of me when I was a kid—particularly before their son was born. Leo was always very nice to me. He used to make me laugh. I can't help remembering all sorts of good things about him. But it would be different for Bumper—he would just see a middle-aged chap under some kind of stress having it off with a girl half his age. During the night there's some kind of trouble—something abnormal sex-wise."

Katie said: "Listen—with sex what's normal?"

"I know. But with a chap of his age ... perhaps she taunted him. I mean, it's possible, something like that, and then he could have lashed out."

"You didn't read a full report of the killing. That girl's head was smashed in with a brass candlestick, a ferocious blow. Not the sort of thing anyone normal would do in a flash of temper."

Buchanan absorbed this unpleasant information silently as they made their way into the vegetarian restaurant. He found it hard to believe that Leo was capable of such a murder, no matter what provocation there had been.

Katie had reached the front of the short queue to the restaurant's counter. "Mm—great!—the vegetable curry is on. It's specially good. I usually have it with mounds of raw mushrooms, tomatoes, cucumber—practically everything they have to offer in fact."

Buchanan followed suit by having his plate piled similarly

high. When they were seated Katie said: "I'm rather intrigued by the girl who turned you down for Inspector Machin. Why did she do that?"

Buchanan grinned. "I like to think that she chose the one she thought would make the better husband, the harder-working, more reliable type, by which I imply a bit of a burke. That's why I always get in a dig about Bumper. You heard me say about him being a belt-and-braces man. I fool myself. Marjorie simply found him more attractive. She had too much sense of humour to be worrying who was most likely to end up with a satisfactory pension."

"She sounds nice."

"She was—undoubtedly still is. Nearly as tall as you, and Bumper too for that matter. Laughed a lot. Large blue eyes, black hair, very nice smile. I heard they have two children. I know that Bumper is doing very well. Detective Inspector is about as good a rank as you can hope for at his age."

"May I ask why you left the police—the second time round I mean?"

"Sure. Simple, really. I had an accident in France." It amused Buchanan to dismiss the time when he had been shot with that phrase. The bullet had passed through his side, leaving a clean uncomplicated wound, but there had been serious haemorrhage and he could easily have died without prompt attention. "It put me in hospital for a while and it happened because I didn't do what I had been ordered to do by a superior officer. So they weren't very pleased. Then there were a few other incidents. I was told that I was not a good team man. It was put to me: 'It's an impersonal business—if you can't accept that then you're just not suited'. I resigned."

"And since then?"

"Nothing very much. I spent some months on the island of Samos helping a young couple to build a *taverna*—laying foundations, general navvying. It was the most satisfying work I've ever done, though that may sound strange."

"Not at all. But Bee said something about you once being a racing-driver."

"For a while. Not a really good one. I knew that I'd never make the grade—very few do. I dropped out. Failure is habit-forming you see."

"Fiddle-de-dee! Nonsense! You just haven't found your niche yet. It's not all that easy."

Buchanan assented silently to the last sentence. It was years since a girl had jollied him along and he had often felt that what he basically lacked was someone to make him stick at things. He saw that while he had been talking Katie had practically polished off her plate of curry—she ate as quickly as he usually did, chewing her food naturally without any finicking self-consciousness. He found both her looks and her easy manner attractive; but his last serious affair had ended up badly, with him feeling a cheat and impostor, half in love with a woman who had fooled him with a story about her husband leaving her when in fact he was dying of leukaemia in Guy's Hospital. This had made him wary about women.

Katie got up, saying: "Will you let me choose a sweet for you? You need to be a habitué here to make the best choice and if we don't grab them soon all the good things will be gone. Okay?"

"Fine. Anything but yoghurt. I've had four months of yoghurt."

He studied her as she waited in the queue by the counter. She had a slight figure but her arms were shapely and very feminine; he was struck again by how attractive a woman's arms could be. He also liked the bouncy way she walked, keeping up with his long strides: all her movements implied a lot of vitality, and she had an enthusiastic, vigorous approach to life. While he was brooding, staring at the back of her neck and the delightful tendrils of curly hair, the colour of which he had decided was not carrot but a blend of red and gold, she turned, holding up two dishes, to catch him staring, and grinned.

84

She came across the room still grinning. "You were very wise to leave the afters to me. I was able to reach across the chap in front, bag the last two cherry puddings and smile sweetly. The sort of thing a woman can do, you see. Like pinching a taxi."

"Looks good."

"Delicious light sponge pudding with black cherries and fresh cream. Can't be bad! Do I sound like the menu in an American restaurant?"

"Yes, you do. But I tend to like someone who likes to eat."

Katie banged into him slightly as she squeezed into the rather awkwardly placed window seat and they looked at each other in silence for a moment before lifting their spoons.

When the puddings were eaten, Katie said: "It's great for Bee you being around. I'll do anything I can for her but she rather needs a strong shoulder to lean on at the moment. It's the combination of being terribly upset and mystified. She can't really think about anything else and of course there's a tremendous amount to do just now. And she's got to decide whether to sell the shop or keep it. You know, you can't get away from the fact that it was a very odd coincidence Sidney Chard going off like that the same day Leo died."

"You knew him, this chap Chard?"

"Yes, quite well. He'd been in the shop fairly often in recent months. Unattractive sort of bloke—middle-aged, balding, with a very aggressive chin, but something about him I admired. He was crippled in the war but it didn't seem to handicap him at all. Quite fantastic energy. He might get hold of a catalogue in the morning post for a sale in Paris and he'd be off within an hour."

"It's possible then that he did go abroad. Perhaps that girl got it wrong about the passport, maybe it was an out-of-date one, something like that."

"He's been gone a month. Very unlike him. Business was his idea of pleasure, not month-long holidays. Besides, there's something else. We know an old dealer called Immanuel Klein who was very fond of Leo. Klein is a sort of runner, you know, he buys things in the country and sells them to West End dealers, doesn't have a shop himself. Well, he's always disliked Sid, would push off in fact if Chard came into our place. The last few times Klein has been round to see me he's hinted that something funny was going on between Leo and Sid, some dodgy kind of business."

"Do you think that's possible?"

"Sid is a bit dodgy—well, sharp, cuts corners shall we say. Not Leo—in fact Leo was too soft really to make much money. He was saved by this flair I told you about. What is definite is that Leo saw a great deal of Sid in the last few months. Became very chummy in fact, used to go round to Sid's flat just off the Tottenham Court Road. Beatrice says he'd known Sid for twenty years, but this close friendship was a very recent thing."

"Okay, I'll try to visit these Alpha Security people this afternoon. Then I'll contact Bumper. Anything else I should know? Nothing about this girl Judy Latimer, I suppose?"

"No, but a bloke I know, Ralph Blencowe, who owns a marine-picture gallery in Homer Street, often goes to a local pub called The Olive Branch at lunch-time. Leo sometimes popped in there for a drink and a sandwich. Ralph said he'd seen this stunning blonde girl with Leo a couple of times. And apparently it was the girl who picked up Leo, not vice versa. Ralph told me that he saw her smiling at Leo, 'giving him the come-on' was how he put it, and then start chatting him up. Ralph also said that he was sure he'd seen the same girl walking along with an unusually handsome young chap— mid-twenties, trendily dressed, silver bracelet. He thought they both looked like models."

"I'll give all this to Bumper. He may have it of course, but a description of that young chap could be useful."

XIII

THE part of Georgian London known as Lincoln's Inn has not been developed nor much tampered with in recent years. The picturesque main portion with its diapered brickwork and sharply pointed windows is there for all to see; those who look a little harder will discover the less ornate north-east corner, near Chancery Lane, where Robert Taylor's Stone Buildings face a later block across a long court.

Strolling up Chancery Lane Ed Buchanan found he had a few minutes to spare before his appointment with Alpha Security and walked through the unprepossessing passage beside No. 76a which leads to the back of a fine arch set on the diagonal. Holborn was a part of London he knew reasonably well, and he had come through this knowledge by his habit of turning down little-used alley-ways.

Star Yard, the address given for Alpha Security's offices, was another such by-way with a bollard set in the passage to make it usable by pedestrians only. Buchanan looked closely at the bollard, wondering whether it had been made from a cannon like those in Upper Thames Street by the side of All Hallows the Less. The Victorian urinal made of cast-iron in elaborate patterns with the royal arms in several panels was worthy of scrutiny too, but a pretty girl was hurrying down the alley and Buchanan did not want to appear like some kind of nut, so he took out the Alpha Security card and studied that instead.

Alpha Security, Bell House (Third Floor), Star Yard, Carey Street, London W.C.2. The address was engraved in large black letters and looked impressive. It seemed a good idea to locate such a business in an enclave of lawyers, and the firm's prompt response to his phone-call had made a good impression. The girl who had answered had spoken in a strange accent that was hard to place, and with a quiet voice, but she had been firm about the time to call being "4.45 precisely".

The name Alpha Security in gilt Roman letters took up little space on the black announcement-board in the entrance hall of Bell House. The names on the other floors were more long-winded, being firms of solicitors that went with the candlestick and sealing-wax, Chancery Court atmosphere of the area. The red rubber floor in the hall was polished enough to skate on in socks and smelt pleasantly of lavender.

There were two doors on the third floor, both bearing the firm's name gilt-lettered in very small italic capitals. One was open and Buchanan walked through it at precisely 4.45 according to his watch and found himself in a small room containing a typist's chromium desk and stool, and two chromium chairs with blue-green seats. The sea-green motif was also found in the highly polished rubber floor which had an embossed wave-like pattern. There were no pictures on the walls and nothing on the desk apart from a phone. The place had an aseptic atmosphere like that of a dentist's surgery, and the clean scent of Eau-de-Cologne.

There were two doors leading out of the small office apart from the one Buchanan entered: on doing so he caught a glimpse of a rather intriguing back view, that of a girl with long black hair, whose disappearance exactly coincided with his entry. Through the other one Buchanan heard a deep voice calling out: "In here. Please come through."

Following these instructions Buchanan found himself in a spacious room with large windows, white walls, sea-green carpet, an oak desk and green leather chairs. A man with thick dark brown hair, about six foot tall, was hunched over a putting-iron, preparatory to tapping a golf ball across the carpet to a gap between two boxes of stationery. The man said "Just a sec" and knocked the ball about ten feet straight through the contrived hole, made a little movement of his head implying satisfaction and turned to greet Buchanan.

He was dressed in a pale brown shirt and trousers of a thin snuff-coloured tweed with a brown overcheck. His brown loafer shoes had the kind of polish that Buchanan had never obtained. He had a handsome face and a sun-tanned complexion, but his small mouth was held fixed in a prissy expression.

The man put down his putter carefully, glanced at his wrist-watch, and said: "You must be Mr. Buchanan. Good. How much easier life would be if everybody kept appointments on time like you and me. Do have a seat." He went to sit behind the large desk. As he did so his pursed lips relaxed into a smile showing perfect teeth. "My name's Richard Madoc, the director here. How can I help you?"

"It was good of you to see me at such short notice." Buchanan noticed that on the wall behind Madoc's head there was a large photograph of a shark on the end of a taut line. He handed over the Alpha Security card, on the reverse side of which Leo Selver had written: "Appointment for June 15th —2.15 p.m." As the card changed hands Buchanan explained: "That date was written by a Leo Selver, so it appears he had an appointment here. Do you remember him?"

Madoc's mouth was pursed again as he shook his head. "You must excuse me—I don't want to appear rude—but how would that concern you? All our clients' business is of course strictly confidential. Without exception."

"Yes, I understand that. But Selver is dead."

"Is he, by God!" Madoc exclaimed, then shot a straight look at Buchanan as if to probe his veracity. "Dead? When was this?"

"About a month ago. The 15th or 16th of August. It was in some of the papers." He extracted the newspaper cutting from the letter he had received from Beatrice Selver and passed it across the desk.

Madoc raised his chin and nodded as he placed the cutting on his immaculate blotter. "Ah yes. Mid August. Well, that explains it. I was off the Scillies then. Catching some of those awful brutes." He pointed over to the large photograph of a shark, then pulled a snapshot from a drawer in the desk. "In fact—it was just about then I had an appointment myself— with this very beast." He pushed the snapshot across the desk's shiny surface, carefully touching only one corner. It showed a shark lying on a beach stretched alongside a row- ing-boat, which was a graphic way of demonstrating its size. "I was exiled on Bryher in a fisherman's cottage, without television, papers or even a wireless." Madoc pushed the news- paper cutting a little further away. "An unpleasant business this. Are you a relative?"

"No, but I'm a friend. I've known the Selvers all my life. Mrs. Selver found the card. You'll understand she's very upset and confused about what happened. And she's puzzled as to why he should have seen you."

Madoc nodded judiciously. "You'll appreciate that if I had indeed been engaged by Mr. Selver and had acted for him, then I could only have divulged such information to the police. In the circumstances, though, I can talk to you. I do remember Selver—he seemed a pleasant chap to me, although our business together was aborted. We had only the one con- versation. He asked my advice about something. I suggested that we could possibly help him, but stipulated a fairly stiff fee. Possibly priced myself out of the market. Frankly we don't care much for the private-detective side of the business now—we're much more concerned in advising firms on security."

"Can you tell me what he consulted you about?"

"He simply told me he thought he was being followed. Wanted to know if we could check up on that. He was obviously suffering from tension. Funnily enough I thought he was in a bad way health-wise. Very taut—pale dry skin— his hands shook."

"Did you believe him—about being followed?"

"Not really. I believed he was worried about something, but followed, no. You see, a whole lot of bods who have come in through that door haven't told me the truth. Possibly I'm oversceptical now. But chaps will so often sit down and outline some vague problem while they're really sizing me up to see if I will tackle something else. One gets to expect it."

"You thought that was the case with Selver?"

Madoc hesitated. "I certainly got the impression he was holding something back. And that, given time enough, he might divulge the real problem. But I'm not a doctor—only like a doctor in that my time is strictly limited. And it has to be rationed, otherwise ..." Madoc underlined all this by glancing at his wrist-watch. As the last sentence petered out he pursed his lips and there was a sudden hint of boredom in his dark brown eyes.

Buchanan got up, saying: "Thanks anyway. I'm grateful. If I hadn't come to see you, Mrs. Selver would have gone on brooding over that card."

Madoc got up too and walked towards the door, saying: "I wish I could have been more helpful. But Mr. Selver was here for, oh, I'd say less than fifteen minutes. No money changed hands. We came to no arrangement. Only that he was to phone for another appointment, if he felt so inclined. He didn't—so that was that. Goodbye, Mr. Buchanan."

"Goodbye. Thank you." Buchanan walked quickly out of the cool faintly scented suite of offices, with a glance at his own watch. He had been allotted exactly fifteen minutes of precious Alpha Security time.

XIV

As the taxi turned down Welbeck Way Katie Tollard said, "Do look!—I love that sign 'Artistes' Entrance'—it's on the back of Wigmore Hall." She declaimed the words "Artistes' Entrance" again in a plummy voice, then knocked on the glass partition to attract the driver's attention. "It'll be fine on the corner, it's very awkward turning round in the mews."

Buchanan could not help wondering about the circumstances under which she had made previous visits to the mews, and whether there had been anything between her and Leo. He handed the driver a fifty-pence piece and got out with his case and various bags. Katie was carrying a parcel of sheets and a rush shopping-basket containing various small items which Beatrice had bought for Buchanan during his trip to Holborn.

Buchanan looked round the mews, at the newly painted Victorian gas-lamp, the urns containing geraniums and hydrangeas, and a gleaming Maserati-Citroën SM parked in front of one garage. "This is certainly your posh London."

As they walked to the front door of No. 3a Katie handed over the key and said: "Yes. Funny about Leo. You know, you'd have thought he had everything he could want. An attractive wife, a good business, this convenient flat and a super country cottage. Have you been there, to the cottage in Hampshire?"

"No, the last time I visited Leo and Bee was about ten years ago, when they lived in Northwood."

"The cottage at Lasham is small but delightful—seventeenth century, oak beams, brick floors, lattice windows, big fireplace in the living-room. Leo ..."

Katie paused as Buchanan opened the door and had not finished what she was saying when they put down their bags in the passage at the top of the stairs.

After a minute Buchanan said: "Will you have a drink? I bought some St. Vincent rum this morning. Should be good. Shall we try it?"

"Just a very small one. I want to pop in on a girl friend who lives in Bentinck Street, then I must get back to Beatrice and tell her you're established here. Do you feel funny about living in this flat?"

"Not really. Bee seemed to want me to. That's all that matters. Besides, it's silly to leave a place like this unused."

"Very sensible. What I was saying about Leo—I mean, he seemed to have everything but—do you know that song—

> Don't it always seem to go that
> You don't know what
> You've got till it's gone?

"Yes, I do. Joni Mitchell's 'Big Yellow Taxi'. Stella, that American girl on Samos, brainwashed me with American folk singers—Joan Baez, Harry Nilsson, Buffy Sainte Marie. I ended up nearly converted."

"All of Leo's records are of the thirties and forties. I suppose really he wanted to go back to that period."

"Yes, I suppose so." Buchanan's chest had begun to ache and he felt that he needed a swig of the Captain Bligh rum. He had enjoyed the evening spent with Beatrice and Katie at the latter's flat in Seymour Street. Katie had dished up a perfect pizza and green salad, and they had drunk two bottles of Beaujolais. He had found it very easy to talk to both of them and had probably talked too much, but suddenly it seemed to have been a long day. Twelve hours after being punched by the bruiser in the wig he was beginning to realise how heavy the blows had been. He had always found alcohol an effective pain-killer. He poured rum into two tumblers.

As she took one, Katie said: "Do you think you'll have any trouble seeing Machin?"

"I don't think so. How much it will achieve is another matter. I can see Bee's point of view, of course, but Bumper may not think it's got much to do with the case he has to solve. It's a strange coincidence about Chard, but it may be just that."

"Perhaps, but Nora Chard's attitude has been so very odd. After all, Leo was quite a friend and he used to make a fuss of their son Clive—yet she hasn't phoned or written to Bee. And the girl I know who works for Sid told me Nora is in a terrible state, quite shaky with nerves, doesn't ever leave her flat although she always used to be out. Most peculiar."

"Bumper couldn't do anything about Mrs. Chard—not if she hasn't gone to the police about her husband being missing ..."

"I'm sure she hasn't. My friend says Nora pretends that everything is okay and yet seems scared stiff. Oh—there was one other thing—Bee and I remembered it when you were in Holborn—another business friend of Leo's, a man called Harry Freedson, phoned Bee twice—and they were rather weird calls. One was just after Leo died. Nora took the call thinking he was phoning just to say how upset he was about Leo, but Freedson went on to ask if there was anything he could do to help. It was strange because Bee didn't know him at all well. Then he phoned a week ago, from Amsterdam, and again asked if there was anything Bee wanted him to do. She thanked him for calling and said no. She was puzzled, said it was like taking a call in code to which she didn't have the key."

"No wonder Bee is bewildered by everything."

Katie finished off her rum. "You won't find much of Leo's stuff here. I collected most of it. Some records are still around, and the record-player, and there's an old mac somewhere. That's about it. The wardrobe and chest-of-drawers are empty. Well, I'll say goodbye."

"Can I see you round to Bentinck Street?"

"Not worth it, thanks, it's only a minute from here. 'Bye Ed. See you tomorrow."

"Goodbye Katie." Buchanan held her arm lightly as they went downstairs. There was a friendly intimacy between them that had sprung up easily and he found it very pleasant. He hoped it might grow into a lasting relationship. He did not want another affair like his last one that had flared up in a sexual passion but had nothing else to support it.

Immediately he had returned upstairs Buchanan picked up the Trim-phone and dialled the number of the Swan Walk flat, letting it ring for a long time. His sore chest and cheek were going to ensure that one day Philip Tureck would hear a rat-tat on his red front door and have to answer some straight questions. Buchanan did not go out looking for trouble, but when it came he believed in retribution on the Old Testament scale. He poured another glass of rum and had a couple of swigs before beginning to put his groceries and clothes away.

Half-way through this chore he walked through to the bed-room and examined the records in the chromium rack. There were a number of Nat King Cole L.P.s and others by Astaire, Crosby, Glen Miller and Sinatra. Apart from the Benny Goodman and Tommy Dorsey discs it was not his kind of music. Again he wondered about Katie's knowledge of the flat. Had she come by it simply in clearing the place up for Beatrice, or had she in fact at some time lain on that bed staring up at the skylight? He did not like entertaining these pawky thoughts about Katie—her relationship with Leo was none of his concern, and such brooding was not his usual style. Probably it had to do with being in the dead man's flat, which seemed to retain something of the stifling atmos-phere of a love-nest rather than a home.

Buchanan walked into the bathroom to wash and clean his teeth. After doing this and switching on the electric heater he was at a loss to know how to pass the time till the water would be hot enough for a bath. He had left his few paper-backs in Samos and there did not seem to be a radio. He refilled his glass with rum and went back to the bedroom, taking out the Tommy Dorsey disc and glancing through the titles of the tunes. Then he put on a Buddy Berrigan single, "Still I can't get started", and idly opened a small corner cupboard to see if he could stow his bags there. It was empty apart from a macintosh and an umbrella hanging on hooks. The umbrella had not been rolled before being put away and Buchanan could see a scrap of blue writing-paper had fallen into the folds. He took out a much creased piece of paper.

There was writing on both sides in Leo Selver's hand. Buchanan sat down on the bed and turned on a small lamp so that he could study it.

On one side there was a list of eleven names under the heading *"Eendracht maakt Macht"* which he could roughly translate as "Unity makes strength":

> Court-Card
> General Sir Claude Everard
> Lord Gleneale—dead
> Lord Robert Montfaucon—dead
> Lord Walmersley—dead
> Sir Oscar Molyneux
> William d'Arfey, M.P.—dead
> Henry Cuyp, M.P.
> Sir Anthony Beddoes—dead
> Brigadier Jack Fitzroy—dead
> Major Hugh Meynell—dead

At the bottom of the list Selver had written: "Of this bunch eight are dead. Henry Cuyp alive, no longer an M.P. but the head of the Arkadie International Corp. Fate of Everard and Molyneux uncertain. Court-Card as much of a mystery today as he was then."

Buchanan stared at this list unable to make any sense of it—he could not remember ever having heard of any of the names. At the top of the other side of the paper Selver had drawn a spider's web. Below it he had written out a quotation:

"Montaigne—

Death is a remedy against all evils: It is a most assured haven, never to be feared, and often to be sought: All comes to one period, whether man makes an end of himself, or whether he endure it; whether he run before his day or whether he expects it: whence soever it come, it is ever his owne, where ever the thread be broken, it is all there, it's the end of the web ..."

96

XV

"... so declare that I will truly serve our Sovereign Lady, The Queen ... without favour or affection, malice or ill-will ... and, while I continue to hold the said office, I will, to the best of my skill and knowledge, discharge of the duties thereof faithfully to the Law; so help me God."

As Buchanan walked over the rustic bridge by the west end of the boating lake in Regent's Park he was going over the Police Oath in his mind. When criticisms had been made of his "not being a good team man", and his tendency to "bend instructions", he had bridled. Now he felt more detached and able to see that what had been said was true. He lacked his father's steadiness and willingness to obey orders even when they seemed stupid—it boiled down to that in the end.

The morning's mist still lay thickly over the lake so that he could hear the quacking of ducks but not see them. There was a pale blue sky and it was going to be the kind of temperate late summer day, with mellow sunlight, that he had sometimes missed during months of unvarying heat on Samos. He glanced at his watch and saw that he was a few minutes early for his meeting with Machin, 9.05 a.m. on Friday, September 14th. The previous day had been passed very pleasantly in Katie's company, even though some of it had been in the alien world of antiques. In the morning he had accompanied her to an auction at the Harrods' rooms in Hammersmith, and found he was interested in the dealers' varying reactions to the sale. They had spent most of the afternoon moving the items she had bought in a self-drive van, and then he had dashed out to Oxford Street to do all his shopping for clothes in half an hour. He intended having the weekend as a holiday and to start looking for a job properly on the Monday.

Standing in a patch of sunlight, he watched the patterns made by a breeze on the surface of the lake and the darting and hovering flight of a dragonfly. The sound of children's laughter tempted him further along the path to a point where he could watch them on the slide and swings in the playground, and see the first young customers taking their seats in small motor-boats.

No sooner had he found a bench in the sun and turned to the page of personal adverts in *The Times* than he heard a familiar voice call out: "Well—if it isn't Mr. Hardnose hissel."

He looked up to see Machin strolling along with a pretty little dark-haired girl. Machin stopped at the gate of the playground, waited till the girl had run across to the swings, then walked over and sat down beside Buchanan.

"Hey up, Ed! What's wi' the man-tan and bleached hair? Eeh, our Marje should see you now!"

"How is she? Still blooming?"

"Aye, she is. Finds it bit 'ard stretching the few pound I gi' her. Any road, you look on your bike again."

"Yes, I'm all right. Is this your day off?"

"Not to worry. Two birds wi' one stone. Our little lad's come doon wi' flu and young Jackie is just ower it—so I'm treating her to a day oot 'fore she goes back t'school. Half an hour here, then it's ower t'planetarium, fish and chips and an ice-cream sundae 'boot a foot high, Madame Tussaud's, home."

A woman who had been pushing a pram sat down on their bench. After a few moments of silence they exchanged glances and got up to walk along the path again. Machin wore a houndstooth check suit, a white shirt with a black and blue tie, and a white mac that appeared brand new. He moved forward in a slightly hunched way, looking down at his feet as if he were playing soccer again and waiting for the kick-off. There was an air of sombreness and tension about him

98

that did not accord with his good looks and immaculate clothes.

"I wanted to see you about Leo Selver. The man found dead in the Stephen Street flat."

Machin stopped walking and looked round directly into Buchanan's face. His expression was plainly derisory. "Private-eye stuff noo eh! Happen you'll be on to more clout nor pudden on that one I reckon."

"Not a chance. Just personal. The Selvers used to be my parents' next-door neighbours. Beatrice Selver ..."

"I'm wi' ye. Nice woman that. Liked her—but t'facts won't change."

"I've got a bit of information you might be able to use."

"Well let's have it then, lad. You know us—we never close."

Buchanan was thinking that Machin had changed a good deal since his early days with the Met. He could remember the time when Bumper's Geordie accent was so thick that some phrases had to be translated—"Howwaydoon tuthe chippy?" meant "Fancy a late snack?" and "Areyegannin doonbye?" was "Are you going down?" Now his accent was much less difficult to understand, with just the occasional homely phrase. The bumptiousness of the youthful soccer star had gone too, replaced by a serious brooding personality which could appear menacing.

"Just that one of Selver's friends, a furniture dealer named Sidney Chard—seems as if he scarpered the same day that Leo died. Hasn't been seen in a month."

Machin's shoulders moved uneasily. "S'nothing to do wi' case, I'll be bound. Mrs. Selver's been on t' me with this kind of stoof. She can't face t'facts ..."

"Chard's going off is a fact, Bumper. We checked again yesterday by phoning his assistant at the shop."

"All reet." Machin took out a notebook and a tiny silver pencil. "Address?"

"S. Chard, Camden Passage. He's in the phone-book with that address and also his flat in Bloomsbury. Mrs. Selver's also had a couple of strange phone-calls from a man called Harry Freedson."

Machin shrugged. "This sort of stoof ... anyone dies ... dig around in their lives ... you come up with stoof you can't explain. You know me, I'm impatient, I like to get a good cough, have everything tied oop reet. But some pieces belong t'noother jigsaw altogether."

"Yes, I suppose so. I just said that I'd pass it on."

" 'Course, Ed. You'll understand I can say nowt."

Buchanan nodded. He knew enough of police work to understand what it must be like to be in Machin's position, up to his elbows every day of his life in the kind of messes that most people would never encounter. He could imagine the police view of the Selver case. The discovery of the macabre bedroom scene by a police constable summoned by a perceptive milkman; the unpleasant details of the two corpses, perhaps strangely discoloured or fouled with excrement; then the intensive work in the flat by the investigating officers and the forensic pathologist. Machin had twelve years' service with the Met., seven of them with the C.I.D.; he was an expert in murder and violent death, knew that seemingly ordinary people under stress were capable of extraordinary acts such as tearing off a woman's face with fingernails or doggedly trying several different painful methods of suicide.

"Well"—Machin fingered his nose thoughtfully—"leastways tell Mrs. Selver I'd say nowt. But I'll tell you one thing, and that is I'm very interested in that Judy Latimer. I can say this as one of the papers got on to it—she was all packed and ready for off. Three suitcases, two bags, three wine-cartons. In fact, everything she owned 'part from the bedroom furniture could have been moved oot of that house in five minutes by taxi. And she had an airline ticket for t'States."

"Christ, I nearly forgot!" Buchanan exclaimed. "There was something else. A bloke called Blencowe who runs an

100

art gallery in Homer Street. It seems he saw Judy Latimer with a young chap, early twenties, trendily dressed. Male model type."

Machin took out his notebook again. "Now you're talking, lad. As the Chief Super says, info regarding that lassie is in short supply. Fact is she's a mystery in herself, like someone picked oot to disappear without trace. An orphan, ye see. Brought up by foster parents in Leicester and it seems they wrote her off years back."

XVI

THE end of the summer is a sobering period for anyone in Ed Buchanan's position. He had passed carefree months doing a job he enjoyed without giving any thought to the future. He had been intoxicated with the sun and sea, and the pleasures of the simple life on Samos. Now he was sobering up, and his hangover took the form of the dreary business of self-evaluation. He felt like the grasshopper in the fable about the industrious ant. He was thirty-one and had failed at two careers, and could not see where he might fit into the scheme of things. He realised that the day-dream of finding another opportunity like the one on Samos was foolish, and he had no wish to spend his whole life navvying. When Stella and Nick had finished their building operations they would have to settle down to the mundane business of running a small guest-house and *taverna*. What kind of work could he settle down to, not for a few months but with the resolve to make it into a career?

Buchanan had lunched well at a French restaurant in Connaught Street with Ken Hughes, the owner of Bathwick Mews Performance Cars. The lunch had been on Hughes and he was always a generous host, particularly with wine, but Buchanan was lucky in that he did not suffer from alcoholic

101

hangovers. It was Hughes' matter-of-fact attitude to Buchanan's prospects that had had a depressing effect. Put simply, Hughes' argument was that Buchanan was well fitted to work for and eventually manage the Bathwick Mews business and was not really equipped for anything else. This was probably true, but Buchanan found it hard to accept. As he walked from Paddington to his meeting with Katie Tollard at Royal Oak station he was trying to think of some form of escape from a lifetime of performance cars.

Hughes had two irritating habits: one was saying "I know what you're thinking"; the other was often being right in his mind-reading act. Hughes had been a much more successful racing-driver than Buchanan, and had taken his winnings and invested them in a business he knew from A to Z. He had a charming wife, three nice kids, a pleasant home in Notting Hill Gate. He never seemed to make a mistake. In one way it would be foolish to turn down his offer.

Walking slowly along Gloucester Terrace, Buchanan mentally listed his own abilities: he was a first-class car mechanic and driver; he could speak a little German and Italian; his French was fluent; he was energetic and not afraid of work. That seemed to be the grand total of things he had to offer in the market-place of employment. He owed his attainments as a racing-driver to his ability to see in slow motion things that were happening at speed, and a capacity to control all his faculties when the unexpected happened, like a cat's ability to fall on its feet or to jump on to an unseen foothold. It was the kind of thing that had enabled him to lose adhesion of the rear wheels of his Porsche Spyder at 140 miles per hour on the Thillois hairpin bend at Rheims, do six revolutions before coming to rest, and be ready to continue the race. Such assets had no commercial value outside the world of motor-racing.

"Hi, there! Ed!"

Buchanan had been walking along looking down at his feet, like Machin, mentally kicking a stone all the way from the entrance of Bathwick Street Mews where he had said goodbye to Ken Hughes. As he turned the corner into Porchester Terrace he looked up to see Katie Tollard running along to meet him. She wore a navy roll-necked pullover and a camel corduroy skirt. With her height and slim figure she always appeared elegantly dressed, though she did not fuss over her appearance. Like Ken Hughes, she seemed to have her life well organised and her priorities all thought out.

"Aren't you though?"

"What?"

"Bee was saying you've never looked so fit. Of course she's prejudiced. I say it's rather a laugh, the idea that you once sat on her lap."

"Absolutely true though. In fact I can remember going to sleep on her lap, or rather I can remember waking up in that position. And very nice it was too. Leo had one of those tiny Austin Sevens in those days, and occasionally we all squeezed in. I don't know how he got it to move."

"What happened with Machin?"

"Nothing much. Told him about Sidney Chard's disappearance but I think he would take a lot of convincing that it has anything to do with Leo's death. Told him about that chap, Blencowe, too, having seen the girl Judy Latimer. Bumper seemed much more interested in that. You can't add anything else about her?"

"You're being discreet—hinting that I might have known something was going on between her and Leo. I didn't. About a year ago I thought he might be having an affair with someone, with a woman who had been a customer. But I never saw Judy Latimer or even heard her name. Of course Leo would have been careful like that. In fact I'm very surprised that he picked her up in our local." She sighed and shrugged. "Well, we'll see what old Manny has to say. Once or twice in the shop I think he's been on the point of blurting something out and then thought better of it because of Bee."

"Did he know Leo very well?"

103

"Yes, he did, in a funny kind of a way. They didn't go out to the pub together, or anything like that. But Manny used to spend a fair amount of time in our shop, loved to have a cup of char and talk over old times in the trade, battles won and lost, the finds he'd made. Still, Manny's not really an egotist, he's very interested in other people and notices things about them. I'm quite sure he's spotted how nervy and irritable Leo had become in recent months. You'll like Manny, you'll find him interesting, and his funny old set-up. Makes marvellous coffee too. Which will be rather welcome. It's been an inky morning."

"Why? More mysterious phone-calls from Freedson?"

"No, nothing dramatic, but we had the accountant round all the morning and that made Bee a bit weepy. Leo wasn't systematic, didn't always keep our stock-book up-to-date, wrote enigmatic little notes on scraps of paper and then lost them. And his cheque stubs! Some with amounts paid but no payee, and some just blank ... Oh, I say! Look down there."

Katie tightened her grip on Buchanan's arm as they reached a grimy plaster pillar in front of a run-down Victorian house with a basement. She pointed down the steps to a window flanked by two dustbins. "Isn't he sweet? Always sits there when he's expecting anyone because he's rather deaf, and the bell's a bit temperamental."

Buchanan saw an old man with a luxuriant beard and spectacles sitting at a small desk close to the window, surrounded by tottering piles of books and magazines. Katie ran down the steps and tapped at the window. The old man put his face right up to the glass, nodded and then turned round. After a few minutes a door round the corner was slowly opened.

When Buchanan had entered the dark basement flat with Katie he understood why the door could not have been opened quickly, for there were more piles of books and cardboard cartons containing books in the passage-way, so that entrance had to be effected cautiously. Katie took the old man's hand, saying in a loud, carefully enunciated way: "This is a friend of Bee's, Manny, Ed Buchanan. He's known Leo and Bee since they lived in the East End, so he pre-dates you even. Ed, this is Professor Immanuel Klein."

Buchanan shook the proffered hand gently. Klein wore an old-fashioned dark-coloured suit with a heavy black silk tie that was knotted about an inch below the gap in his stiff collar; a watch-chain was strung across his waistcoat. He had wiry black and white hair which merged indivisibly with a beard of similar badger colouring, so that he seemed to peer out through chinks in a bristly hedge. Behind thick lenses his pale brown eyes had a sad expression that reminded Buchanan of Machin. It struck him forcibly how much concentrated experience Machin must have had of unpleasant duties, breaking news of deaths, questioning relatives, looking at corpses. It was no wonder that Bumper's one-time cheerful expression had been replaced by a look that was wary and sombre.

Klein said: "Welcome! Welcome, my dears! Katie is used to all this chaos but you'll find you have to pick your way I'm afraid, Mr Buchanan. My business ..."

Katie brushed this aside briskly: "You're not to run yourself down, Manny. It's a good business. You get some fine things."

"My business?" Klein paused and half-turned round. He gave a short, gasping laugh. "My business is grasping at straws. Every week I need a little miracle."

Buchanan could not remember ever having entered a room so cluttered with a multitude of things; there were so many that it was impossible to take them in. He stared around, pondering the quirks of personality that drove him to dislike possessions and Klein to hoard them. It seemed as if Klein hoped to re-create a world that he had lost. Two walls were covered with framed photographs, some of them sepia-coloured and looking a hundred years old. There were also

105

numerous framed prints and German posters. A third wall was lined with shelves crammed with books and magazines. There were so many piles of papers and oddments on the floor that Buchanan found it difficult to move without creating further disorder. He sat down on a fragile-looking chair as soon as Katie had found space on a sofa with springs broken by its load of box-files and brown paper parcels. In one corner of the room there was an antiquated gramophone with a horn, and a radio that looked nearly as old in a wooden case with a fretsaw design. A coffee percolator was bubbling away on a gas-ring.

Klein slowly turned the chair by the desk round to face his visitors and sat down with a sigh. He addressed Katie, making a gesture of inadequacy: "Would you, my dear? The coffee? I get so flustered with guests. I do absurd things."

"Of course, Manny."

Klein fiddled with a thick pencil, half opening his mouth as if to say something and then rejecting it. Katie, handing round the coffee, seemed to hover in alert speculation, unwilling to break in on his concentration. When she was seated Klein said: "I've been hoping for a good talk with you, my dear. Certain things I did not like to say in front of Mrs. S. That terrible business about Leo. Never will I believe he killed the girl. That is an inexplicable mystery." He turned to scrutinise Buchanan, saying to Katie: "Does our friend here understand about our funny old business—I mean, such technical data as the Ring, settlements, that kind of thing?"

"No, I don't. I spent just one day at Harrods' auction rooms with Katie, and that was the only sale I've attended."

Klein nodded gravely, picked up a pamphlet from the desk and held it by one corner, waggling it back and forth: "Just after Easter this year I went to a small sale at Launceston. That's near Bodmin Moor in Cornwall. Three London dealers formed a Ring at that sale. Five months later one of them is dead, one has disappeared, and the other has shut up his shop and gone abroad."

106

"That was the Trewartha sale?" Katie asked.

"Correct. Property of the late Marquess Trewartha, last of the line, who died in December 1972."

"The elaborate black leather harness in the window at Crawford Street came from the Trewartha collection, Ed. And that massive iron fireback with the coat of arms."

Klein turned to face Buchanan squarely as he explained: "A Ring is an arrangement by which dealers gang together at an auction, appoint one of their group to do all the bidding, then hold another auction, a 'knockout', among themselves afterwards. The difference between the prices realised at the proper auction and the 'knockout' is split up between the dealers unsuccessful at the second sale. That is the 'settlement'. Quite illegal, this sort of thing, but it still operates occasionally. Of course the law is hard to uphold in such matters. I've never been a member of the Ring but you can understand the temptation to come to some kind of arrangement between dealers. For example, supposing Katie and I were the only dealers to attend a small sale. Should we bid each other up or should we come to some arrangement beforehand about abstaining from bidding on some lots? You see?"

Katie pulled a face. "Leo didn't like settling. If he did it was because of Sid Chard."

Klein said: "You're right. The three London dealers in the Ring were Leo, Mr. Chard and Harry Freedson from Highgate. They had no real opposition. The weather was terrible, the catalogue was a bad one, and very few people attended the sale—mainly farmers' wives, a doctor who only wanted a picture and a sundial, and yours truly. The Ring kindly allowed me to purchase six minor items. They took all the good things."

Katie said: "I didn't know that Sid and Freedson had attended the Launceston sale. Our lots came up by carrier, apart from the harness and two clocks which Leo brought back in his car. I do remember Leo saying he'd taken a run out to the Trewartha Place ruin and that it was the bleakest, most inaccessible house he'd ever seen. Apparently, it's right on the moor surrounded by bogs and streams, with hills at the back. When I was doing some research to write up the harness I came across a newspaper report of Trewartha's death, and it said that no one had seen him for ten years before the fire though that hardly seems possible."

Klein waved the sale catalogue. "It hardly seems possible that something should happen to all three men who formed the Ring. In just five months! Where is Mr. Chard? I dislike that man but I do not know anyone in the trade who is harder-working. Making money is his religion. What is he doing, leaving his business for a month? And why has Harry Freedson closed his shop and gone to Holland?"

"Bee's had two odd phone-calls from Freedson, vaguely hinting that he's in a position to help her," Katie said.

"You see? Of course there's some great mystery here. It seems, my dears, that for once I was very fortunate in not being admitted to the Ring." Klein flicked through the pages of the catalogue. "I've looked through this countless times but there's no clue I can find, I'm sure there's nothing here of exceptional value."

"May I borrow the Trewartha catalogue, Manny?" Katie asked. "Leo told me he hadn't kept his copy because the entries were worthless."

"Of course, my dear, keep it for as long as you wish. I've an absurd feeling about this matter, so absurd that I hardly care to admit it. But it seems as if there must be a curse on the Trewartha property."

"The fire destroyed the house completely?" Buchanan asked.

"Only the stone shell remained. I talked to the auctioneer's clerk about it, and he said that a postman spotted the flames and tried to get in through a window but was beaten back. By the time the fire-engine got there most of the roof had fallen in. Then the hoses brought the fire under control and the firemen carried out some things that were in the hall and a small study near the front door. They searched for Trewartha but his body wasn't found till the next day. A strange, lonely death for a strange man."

XVII

THE King of Diamonds in the Greek pack of playing cards was dressed in a multi-coloured robe and carried a spear, the letter B and a diamond surmounted by a crown were placed in the corners of the card. The Queen wore a similar robe, her double image being bisected by a lily. The Jack of Diamonds was dressed like a warrior in classical times, holding a helmet.

Buchanan nad opened the pack of cards that he had bought in Athens with the idea of playing Patience, but the King of Diamonds reminded him of the phrase written by Leo: "Court-Card as much of a mystery today as he was then". He sorted out all the court-cards and laid them in a row across Leo's kitchen table. A small printed slip of paper fluttered from the carton on to the floor and Buchanan picked it up realising he did not know whether it was a manufacturer's guarantee or a ticket in a sweepstake. It was absurd to have worked for four months on a Greek island and end up knowing only a few tourist phrases. "You're not trying", Stella Messisklis had often said in commenting on his lack of concentration when they had puzzled together over the Greek language, but had been ready to excuse it because of his long hours of manual work. Buchanan found it harder to excuse: he knew that he often did shy away from thinking things out or applying himself to a problem. Sitting alone in the Welbeck Street Mews flat he decided that for once, if only for half an hour, he would really concentrate on the mystery surrounding Leo Selver and see what that would achieve.

He went into the bedroom and took a pad of writing-paper from his battered suitcase. He had spent most of the day in Katie Tollard's company and they had talked about various points concerning Leo Selver—it would be interesting to see if they formed more of a pattern when written down in chronological order.

Returning to the kitchen he put on a kettle to make some instant coffee. The afternoon and evening had been spent very pleasantly with Katie, and he had enjoyed walking round Hampstead, an area she knew much better than he did, but their evening meal in Highgate had been a poor one, with rough wine and weak coffee. He intended to blot out the memory with a good strong brew and the remains of the Captain Bligh rum.

After the first sip of coffee he began to write, taking more trouble than he usually did in order to set out the facts clearly:

On Wednesday April 25th 1973, two days after the Easter holiday, Leo Selver attended an auction in Launceston at Whelan's Rooms, Hill Street. The sale was of the surviving contents of Trewartha Place. With his friends Sidney Chard and Harry Freedson, Selver formed a "Ring". Purchases for the "Ring" were all made by Sidney Chard, who bought some ninety-five items out of the total of two hundred.

Manny Klein had noted down the purchaser's names in his copy of the catalogue, marking Chard's lots as "C". Klein appeared certain that the sale did not include anything of exceptional value. It seemed that Leo Selver had subsequently purchased thirty items at the "knockout" after the sale: this was the number that went into the stock at the Crawford Street shop; of these only four now remain unsold. After the Trewartha sale Selver's relationship with Chard seems to have changed. "They became like conspirators" was the phrase used by Klein. Very brief biography of Lord Trewartha, who died in December 1972, in *"Who's Who"*: TREWARTHA, 10th Marquess of, cr. 1690; Charles James Everett; b. 17 Mar. 1907; son of 9th Marquess and Jane Edith (d. 1930), d. of Sir James Walters. Educ.: Eton; Balliol. Address: Trewartha Place, Cornwall.

Apart from the change in his relationship with Chard, Selver became a much more nervous character in the months following the sale, "irritable, unsettled, unable to concentrate and doing little work in the shop" according to K. On June 15th he went to see a private detective, apparently concerned about the possibility that he was being followed. On the 17th August Selver's dead body, together with that of the girl Judy Latimer, was discovered in her ground-floor flat in Stephen Street.

Buchanan's rare mood of concentration was broken by the sound of a car driven at speed into the mews, followed by a vigorous tooting and, moments after, the ringing of the doorbell. As he came downstairs he could see through the frosted glass at the top of the door that the caller looked like Katie.

On opening the door he saw a much more glamorous version of the windswept girl he had said goodbye to only an hour or so previously, dressed in black velvet trousers and a white and gold pullover with a cowl collar. Her hair was arranged differently and she was wearing eye make-up.

"Hello Ed. Do you mind being called out like this?"

"You must be joking." Buchanan gestured vaguely round the mews. "Knock on any door and see if you get complaints." He stepped outside and shut the door behind him. "Does that answer your question? You've done something to your hair. I'm not sure what but I like it."

"Do I still look pale?"

Buchanan thought: I couldn't have said that—correction I could have said that. He was so intent on keeping his relationship with Katie different from his last affair that he had made the mistake of treating her too much like a friend instead of an attractive girl. "Difficult to say in this light but I should say, yes, a little pale. Pale but lovely. Very lovely."

Without being aware that either of them had moved forward they were kissing and their first kiss was as exciting as he thought it might be.

When she stepped back Katie looked at him in silence for some moments and then said: "Well, that's nearly made me forget why I came. But I'm glad I did. I was going to ask if you would pop round with me to Homer Street. Ralph Blencowe, the art dealer, did some detective work himself. He spotted a fashion photograph of that young bloke he saw with Judy Latimer, phoned the *Sunday Times*, in which it appeared, tracked down the advertising agency and finally came up with the young man's name. He's called Toby Crest —apparently he's one of the male models most in demand at the moment and has been working in New York for a few weeks. Now he's back here and"—Katie glanced at her watch—"at this minute, with any luck, should be at Homer Street."

"Okay, let's go then. I shan't change because I know I can't compete with glamorous male models."

Katie got into her black Mini saying: "Fool. I didn't get dressed up like this to impress Master Crest—it's just that Blencowe has this very lovely girl friend Sandy and I thought I must make an effort."

Buchanan studied her in profile as they turned into Welbeck Way and then Welbeck Street. Her driving was so good that he could completely relax in her car, which was unusual for him. She looked round and smiled. "There's a kind of party going on at Homer Street, but then there nearly always is. I mean, most evenings Blencowe seems to have people round. He's quite successful, makes a lot of money and appears to want to spend every penny. Yes, bottles start being opened very early in the evening chez Blencowe. 'We'll warm up the ice-cubes' is his usual greeting. He was married with kids

112

but the wife went off, beautiful Sandy appeared, and now it's live-today-and-forget-tomorrow. Anyway you'll see. Oh yes, there's something else. While we were walking round Hampstead Heath poor Bee had two more phone-calls from Freedson in Amsterdam. Now, apparently, he's quite frantic about there being something he must give to her, wants her to go to Amsterdam on Monday."

"If she doesn't fancy that I'll go for her," Buchanan said quickly. "I'm keen on getting this mystery unravelled, I like flying trips, I like Amsterdam, I'd like to meet Harry Freedson for that matter. Yes, I'd gladly go if Bee wants me to."

"I'm sure she would. At the moment she doesn't know what to say. She's pulled both ways but mostly she's scared. It would be marvellous if you could go."

"Monday I shall still be unemployed. It's on Tuesday the queue of would-be employers will appear."

"Don't sell yourself short, Ed. There's plenty of time. We can think about it."

Buchanan looked round at her quickly at the mention of the crucial pronoun and she looked back smiling. He felt foolishly happy at the idea of being considered as a partner by Katie, it opened up all kinds of possibilities, gave him a more positive outlook. He'd been a loner too long and was sick of it. Suddenly she laughed. "God, this kind of thing is damaging to one's sense of direction. I work in this area, I live here, I should know the bloody one-way system by now. So how did I get lost?"

Buchanan had been oblivious of where they were, but glancing round he recognised Marylebone Road. Katie pulled up and said: "Probably risky doing this with an ex-copper but I'm going to back into a one-way the wrong way."

She parked the Mini in front of a row of cars which practically filled Homer Street. The Marine Gallery showroom was only faintly lit from the stairs at the back of the shop but lights were on in two of the floors above, pop music was blasting from an open window, and as they got out of the car they heard the sound of a glass being smashed followed by loud laughter. Katie raised her eyebrows. "Sounds as if the ice-cubes started being warmed up early tonight. Still, Ralph's a nice bloke. He wouldn't have bothered to track down Master Crest otherwise. You see, he's got a soft spot for Bee like a certain other character I know."

Blencowe's party had spilled down the stairs into the shop and one couple were engrossed in each other on a settle in the corner of the unlit gallery. They did not move when Buchanan tapped on the glass door, but after a few moments a short plump man hopped clumsily over another couple sitting on the bottom stair and came across to let them in. He approached the door with great care like a man told to walk a straight line at a police-station. He was about thirty-five, with an amiable expression, the foundations of a paunch, and eyes that did not seem to focus properly though he was able to recognise Katie, breathing a wine-smelling "Hello darling" and kissing her cheek. For the first time in his life Buchanan experienced a pang of what he supposed must be jealousy.

Once they were in the gallery Katie said: "Ralph Blencowe —Ed Buchanan." She seemed to be faintly amused by Blencowe, watching him as if he was doing a funny turn that might well become funnier.

Blencowe blinked a few times as he stared at Buchanan, seeming to have focusing trouble again with his protuberant eyes and leaning forward at a precarious angle. "Hello! hello! So glad that you could come. Most welcome."

Katie said: "Ralph! There was a special reason. Don't say you've forgotten."

" 'Course didn't ... forget. Never ... forget anything. Crest's here all right." The words were slurred and appeared to be the product of great concentration. "He's ... two floors up at a ... guesstimate. Remarkably handsome ... self-possessed

114

young man ... must say. Seems to be ... more at home here than I am. Have a little drink."

There was a table covered with bottles and glasses placed strategically near the bottom of the stairs so that taking a drink seemed to be a compulsory practice on entering, like taking off shoes in a mosque. Blencowe picked up a bottle of champagne and sprayed it liberally over three glasses.

Katie raised her glass as if proposing a toast. "Thanks, Ralph. It was good of you. Bee's very grateful." Then she raised it again in Buchanan's direction and Buchanan, responding, knew the gesture had a secret significance for both of them.

Blencowe swayed forward a little and said: "Yesh, by all means ... lesh find Crest. Sure he'll make us all feel ... quite welcome." He gulped down his champagne, put his glass on the table with exaggerated care and began to ascend the stairs, lifting his feet too high for the risers, displaying the stolid concentration of someone drunk and vague as to what he was doing. The first floor they came to was packed tight with an overflow of dancers from a large room erratically lit with brilliant coloured lights and images of silent movie films flickering on a white wall. The would-be dancers, jigging about to the Pink Floyd disc "Dark Side of the Moon", were too crowded to make more than a show of movement. They were a modishly-dressed bunch and seemed to Buchanan to include a large percentage of upper-class characters, the kind who sometimes appear to be disguised as half-wits. Unable to move at all for some moments, Buchanan watched comic images of Charlie Chaplin being replaced by those of a doomed airship bursting into flames projected on the wall at the end of the room, and picked up snatches of conversation.

"Upstart!"

"Upshut."

"Temper, temper!"

"Bring your muscles then."

"Just try that on for size."

Blencowe turned round, his face glistening in the fitful flashes of bright light, saying confidentially: "S'not here. Was upstairs ... think ... talking to Sandy."

They made slow progress through the dancers and couples sitting on the stairs to the next floor, where another large room was much less crowded, with dim conventional lighting and a record-player which was in the process of changing a French disc to one of Bobby Darin singing "My Buddy":

> Miss your voice, the touch of your hand
> Just long to know you understand
> Your Buddy misses you ...

Katie exchanged an amused glance with Buchanan. Being quite sober and not in a party mood they shared a feeling of detachment, like visitors to an institution. Blencowe stood in the doorway, swaying slightly, with a solemn expression, beckoning to one of the dancers. Buchanan thought that Blencowe's finger pointed in the direction of two twin-like glamorous girls dancing together, but a moment later a tall young man dressed in a bomber jacket made of bleached calico with steel buttons, matching trousers and a navy-blue turtle-necked pullover came out of the room.

Blencowe blinked several times, made a fuddled introduction and then hesitated, looking as if he might be going to do it all over again.

Katie put out her hand to be shaken and said: "Thanks for coming. I worked for Leo Selver ... the man who was found with Judy Latimer. We're still very puzzled by all of it. No one seems to know anything about Judy. Did you know her well?"

The young man in the calico suit was unnaturally good-looking. His eyes were a pure green colour, like those of a cat, unusually large and with long black lashes. Buchanan did not generally notice much about a man's appearance but it was difficult not to take in Crest's gleaming teeth and glossy

116

blond hair. He had a strong jaw and a firm sharply-defined mouth which acted as a kind of antidote to his feminine eyes. He gazed intently at Katie and Buchanan on first seeing them but then appeared to lose interest. When Katie asked her question he shrugged.

"No, not well. Somehow I doubt if anyone knew her well. At least, that's the impression I got of her."

Crest turned to look directly at Buchanan. "Are you with the police?"

"No, but you'll have to see them."

"Oh God, that's just what I don't need at the moment, getting involved with the noddies. I've got this trip to Hong Kong coming up. And it's important."

Buchanan knew he could no longer perform at "ten tenths" in a Formula One car, but he was equally sure that his perceptiveness about people had never been keener. He prided himself on an ability to observe things that were revealing— involuntary gestures, sighs, flashes of malice. With Crest he felt baffled: it was like tuning into a wireless broadcast and getting a jumbled signal. His face was like a handsome mask; he was unusually self-possessed and still; it was impossible to think of him making a nervous gesture.

Buchanan said: "No reason why they should take up much of your time. Probably just a few minutes to get some background information. Apparently her landlord and the neighbours in Stephen Street knew next to nothing about her. The police found out she had foster parents in Leicester, but that was a blind alley because they hadn't seen her for some years."

Crest nodded at this, then motioned that they should walk along to the end of the passage where no one else was standing. Katie and Buchanan did so but Blencowe, blinking rapidly, began to walk cautiously back towards the stairs.

"Those awful people in Leicester were a lot to blame— I mean, for Judy being so mixed-up and insecure. She looked good so people got the wrong impression. Really she lacked

117

all confidence in herself. Could be built up in a moment. Or destroyed just like that, say the wrong word to her. Apparently that chap in Leicester fancied her, tried something on a couple of times, and his wife was jealous. That's why Judy ran away to London. She hated 'Uncle Jack', got nervous if she even spotted anyone who looked like him. She was always talking about going abroad where he couldn't follow her."

"Did you know she was going? Had her bags packed in fact."

Crest's Adonis-like face still served as a mask. He hesitated for a moment but Buchanan was unable to tell whether it was because he was considering the matter or preparing a lie.

"No, but I'm not surprised. It was an obsession of hers, this idea that her troubles would all end if she could only get to the Eldorado they call New York. An illusion of course." His tone indicated his strictly neutral attitude to other people's hopes and illusions.

Katie regarded Crest coolly; with him she seemed unable to produce her normally friendly manner. "Did she ever mention Leo to you?"

This time Crest did not hesitate. "No. But then she hardly ever talked about personal matters to me. I spotted her once with a Chinese girl, otherwise she always seemed to be on her own. We worked together earlier this year, that's how I met her. You know the kind of thing, posing on a beach in Torquay in March, pretending that we were basking by the Mediterranean. While we were shivering and waiting for the sun to come out we discovered that we lived about five minutes from each other. I used to bump into her shopping in Goodge Street. We had a drink a couple of times. She chatted about jobs, the scarcity of jobs, and of being hard up. That's about it. What on earth can the police make out of that?" Crest looked back up the passage. For a moment it looked as if he had already forgotten what they were talking about.

"About jobs?" Buchanan asked. "Do you know who she worked for recently?"

"A crummy joint called the Blue Eyes Studios, in Greek Street. They specialise in those dreary naughty-nightie ads, the terrible black-net jobs which are supposed to provoke failing husbands. Shouldn't be surprised if they didn't make the odd skinflick there too. Awful dump. But then Judy wasn't having much luck. She had to take what she could get." Crest patted his pockets as if searching for cigarettes and said "Poor Judy" in an absent way. There was an unmistakable aura of boredom about him, as if he had been let into the Secret of the Universe and found out it was not very interesting. "Was there an inquest?"

"Adjourned. Till two weeks from now. Westminster Coroner's Court." Katie gave Crest another cool, appraising look as she said this.

"What about—I mean, what happened to the body?"

"University College mortuary."

Buchanan added an explanation. "In cases of murder the body belongs to the State till the police inquiries are finished. Relatives don't get possession of the body till that time, when it is released to them with a letter from the Home Office."

"Ed was with the police," Katie said, as though giving his account authority.

Buchanan thought: That is the kind of introduction I can do without. Anyone hearing it would ponder the verb "was" and probably not give him the benefit of the doubt. But he knew why Katie had mentioned it, to try to prop up Crest's decision to see the police. He said: "If you go along to the Tottenham Court Road station tomorrow, I'm sure you'll find the matter will be dealt with promptly Can't think that it need interfere with any of your travel plans."

"All right. I'll do that then. Shall I mention seeing you?"

"They won't have heard of me. Just say you want to see Inspector Machin regarding the dead girl found in the Stephen Street flat."

119

"Okay. Now I think I could use another drink." Crest looked at Katie to see if she would join him but she shook her head as she smiled faintly, saying: "Right then. Well, thanks again for coming here. Perhaps we'll see you later?"

"Fine." Crest seemed satisfied with this vague arrangement. His mouth twisted into an actor's flashing grin but his eyes remained cold. He walked away quickly towards the room where dated, smoochy music was being played.

Buchanan was struck by the odd feeling that Crest had given them a vital clue about the Selver mystery, but a moment later his mind hopped nimbly away from this intuitive sensation and he began to review the banal information they had been given about Judy's foster parents, Crest's first meeting with Judy in Torquay, the Blue Eyes Studio in Greek Street.

Katie whispered: "What a cold fish! Poor Judy indeed! A lot he cares. How about ending up with Master Crest as your best friend? Quite a character, Mr. Narcissus."

"Very good-looking."

"Oh yes. Beautiful in fact—but rather frightening really. Like that boy in the fairy-tale about the Snow Queen, the one who got the snowflake in his eye. Heartless. Do you think he'll go and see Machin?"

"I should think so. He'd be very foolish not to now he's told us."

Buchanan smiled at Katie and put his arm round her as they walked along the passage and down the stairs to find Blencowe, but he was still considering the scant information they had been given and pondering his strange intuition.

XVIII

WHEN Ed Buchanan arrived in Amsterdam, "the city of bells and bicycles", it was raining hard. There had been an ominous pall of grey cloud at Schiphol Airport stretching across the

Zuider Zee, now renamed Ijsselmeer, but the large drops did not start to fall till the KLM bus entered the city terminal in the Museumplein.

In his brief motor-racing period of affluence Buchanan had stayed in Amsterdam at the Amstel and the Krasnapolsky: travelling at Beatrice Selver's expense, he had decided to spend the night in a more modest hotel he had once spotted in the Leidsegracht. It had been his original plan to fly in and out of the city in one day, leaving only a few hours to collect whatever it was that Harry Freedson considered to be so important or precious. The plan had been changed during the course of Sunday and three long telephone calls from Freedson to Beatrice, calls in which Freedson at first refused to hand the treasure over to anyone apart from Bee and then gradually came round to dealing with Buchanan after having been given profuse assurances about his trustworthiness. Even so, Freedson had been unwilling to make a definite appointment for a meeting or to divulge his address in Amsterdam. The only firm arrangement he would make was that Buchanan should call in at the office of a Mr. H. V. de Kort, a lawyer whose business address was on the Keizersgracht.

Amsterdam came high on the list of Buchanan's favourite cities and it was not necessary to twist his arm to persuade him to prolong his trip. On previous visits he had seen a few of the touristic "places of interest" but he had spent happier hours mooching round the old Jordaan area, and he hoped to revisit it once the business with Freedson was concluded. Even the light in the Jordaan seemed to be grey and something indefinable from bygone centuries lingered there, where hundreds of little houses were packed closely together and the Jordaners called each other "Uncle" and "Aunt", keeping up a close-knit community tradition; where you could hear accordion music and quavery old voices singing in the café *"De Twee Zwaantjes"*.

After booking a room for the night at the Hotel De

121

Leydsche Hof, and receiving a welcome that would put many British hotels to shame, Buchanan set out to get a snack before calling at de Kort's office. Despite the steady rain he was already enjoying his trip. The Dutch said the British were something like them, having lost an empire and kept a monarchy and a taste for beer; Buchanan felt there were other more important links but he had a taste for beer and was looking forward to a glass of it with a sandwich.

Once he had started walking along the canals his eyes were continually taken by the different gables on the merchants' houses, a shop selling rag dolls and puppets, a street-organ brilliantly painted with peacocks, roses and stars. The delicious smell of coffee being ground attracted him to a "brown café" on the Singel where he ordered a *broodje ros*, a sandwich of thin slices of rare roast beef in a bun, and a light Pils beer.

Eating this modest lunch, he had wry thoughts of his last trip to the city when he had been accompanied by a French girl who was an enthusiast of motor-racing, good food and sex. They had stayed at No. 1 Professor Tulpplein, and three days had been passed largely in making love, with breaks for splendid meals at the Oesterbar and the Restaurant Dorrius. There had been time for one interlude at the Jordaan festival, seeing the funfair on the Palmgracht, listening to music in the brilliantly lit side-streets and dancing on one of the illuminated barges on the Brouwersgracht, but generally it had been a kind of sex and food marathon from which Jacqueline had emerged undisputed winner, with unabated appetite.

Drinking a cup of coffee Buchanan's thoughts became more serious, turning again to the Leo Selver affair. When Katie had driven him to London Airport he had spotted an inscription in whitewash on a wall, in letters at least a foot high: THE FAR AWAY IS CLOSE AT HAND. He had been struck by how apt this was concerning Selver's death. Leo must

122

have entered Judy Latimer's flat in a happy mood, excited at the prospect of making love to the girl; yet within a few hours they were both dead. Could there really be some connection between their deaths and whatever it was that "the Ring" had purchased at the Trewartha sale? And was there a link also with the list of distinguished-sounding names that Leo had made together with his verdict on their fate: "Of this bunch eight are dead. Henry Cuyp alive ... Court-Card as much of a mystery today as he was then."

Strolling along the Singel, looking at the flower market, Buchanan found it hard to believe that probably within an hour or so he was going to be given an explanation of what had happened by the talkative Harry Freedson. Volubility was a quality that Katie had stressed in her description of Freedson. "Short, thin, with dark hair and eyes. Intelligent, nervy, sees the funny side of things. Gestures a lot and it's hard to stop him talking, but I like him." Buchanan did not care how much Freedson would talk—any conversation with him was bound to be fascinating in the circumstances. His steps quickened as he turned into the Keizersgracht.

H. V. de Kort's address was an impressively large house, newly decorated and redolent of prosperous activities within. There was a short flight of steps up to the tall, heavy wooden door which was slightly ajar. The hall had a floor of black and white squares, made out of highly polished rubber and looking like a giant chess-board. On a door to his right he saw the names "Mr. H. V. de Kort, Mr. J. K. Stuyt—Advocaten en Procureurs", and pressed a gleaming brass bell.

The door was opened by a tall blonde with a delectable-looking mouth that turned up at the corners like Katie's. She smiled so nicely that Buchanan experienced a fleeting sensation of pleasurable anticipation despite the fact that his philandering days were over. He smiled back and asked: "Do you speak English?"

"Oh yes. Some."

"Good. My name's Buchanan. Mr. Harry Freedson suggested that I should call in here today. He said he would tell Mr. de Kort to expect me."

The smile vanished and there was just a suggestion of a frown as the girl said, "Oh yes. Please sit down", pointing to a chair close to her desk. She touched a red telephone, saying *"Hebt U een pas?"*, then "Sorry. Do you have any identification? Your passport?"

Buchanan handed her his passport and an international driving licence. The girl flicked open the passport to check on his photograph and took it with her as she left the room, saying: "Only a moment. There are magazines on the table."

Buchanan did not feel like reading. A sensation of excitement was growing in him as he approached the meeting with Freedson, and he knew it would be impossible to concentrate on any printed matter.

The interior door opened within a minute and the attractive blonde appeared again, closely followed by a man in his mid-fifties dressed in a grey flannel suit and white shirt with a dark blue tie. He was an urbane figure, with well-groomed silver hair and an easy smile. He held out his right hand to shake Buchanan's and passed back the driving licence and passport.

"Good afternoon, Mr. Buchanan. I'm Herman de Kort. Harry asked me to stroll along with you." He turned to the girl saying: "Half an hour, Godi. Tell Skemper I can see him at about three."

De Kort took a dark blue raincoat and a brown felt hat from the rack and said to Buchanan: "You don't worry about the rain? Won't you get soaked?"

"No, I'll be all right."

"Ah, what it is to be young! When you get to my age circumspection sinks in. And the rain does too. But then, Dutch rain is special, rather like our own character—stolid, dogged."

Buchanan waved goodbye to the girl and walked out of

124

the office after de Kort who was brooding on his last sentence with obvious dissatisfaction. "Not stolid, dogged. No, they're not the right adjectives for rain. What should it be?" He pushed open the front door, gesturing towards the wet street.

Buchanan suggested, "Steady, persistent?" and then grinned, adding, "I find it funny. I mean that you should be so concerned about getting the adjective exact. Imagine someone in London able to do the same thing in Dutch."

De Kort shrugged. "That's how it is for us, how it has always been, we *have* to learn languages. Is this your first visit to Amsterdam?"

"No, my fifth, and I think it rained on each of my other trips so it hasn't taken me by surprise. I just don't own the right sort of clobber."

"Well, if it's your fifth, presumably you like it here."

"I do, very much. It's a city like Edinburgh—I keep on seeing places where I think it would be nice to live. A flat on any of the quieter canals would suit me fine. I like the atmosphere here too, the friendliness and tolerance. And if you are stolid and dogged, aren't they good qualities? That was shown in the war, wasn't it? Trying to resist the Nazis, trying to hide the Jews?"

De Kort said: "You mustn't paint too rosy a picture of us. I could add a few warts. Before the war there was a large fascist group here. Indeed, I can remember standing on the edge of one of their party meetings and feeling sick, quite desperate in fact. I put that in just to keep the balance. Certainly we had our heroes too, the dockers, the women who starved themselves in '45 to give their children food, men like the writer Johan Huizinga willing to be deported as hostage at the age of seventy ... Yes, you're right after all, we're not a bad lot. A bit dull perhaps."

Threading a way through busy traffic on the Spui and dodging round a three-carriage tram broke up the conversation. Despite the rain the Kalverstraat was crowded with shoppers, most of whom seemed to be under twenty-five.

Somewhere an organ was grinding out endless variations on "Tulips from Amsterdam".

Buchanan guessed they were heading in the general direction of the Zeedijk, the sailors' area near the Oosterdok, where you could get cheap beer and food, and lots of trouble if you didn't watch your step.

As if in answer to the question Buchanan had phrased only mentally, de Kort came to a halt outside the Galerie Mokum in the Grimburgwal, saying: "Despite my dogged, resolute steps I'm not quite sure yet of our destination. That's Harry for you. I suggested he should use my office for the meeting. But that was too simple for him. So now you must just wait a moment while I check again. However, it's a nice spot. This is the famous 'House on the three canals'. Do you mind waiting here?"

Buchanan said: "Not at all."

De Kort crossed over two small bridges and stepped into a glass cubicle lettered *"telephoon"*. An old woman carrying two shopping-bags saw Buchanan sheltering in the shop doorway and gestured with her head at the grey sky, saying: *"Het regent altijd"*. As if to meet this challenge the rain faltered and a few moments later came to a stop. Immediately it did so a canary began to chirp.

Buchanan stepped out of the doorway and stared up at the gradually lightening sky. To the north above the area of warehouses and islands there was a widening streak of washed-out blue. The break in the weather had come just in time to prevent his being soaked. The heavy brown boots which he had bought in Samos would stand up to any amount of rain, but his shoulders were beginning to feel decidedly damp and the windbreaker jacket was clinging to his back in places.

De Kort came striding back over the nearest bridge with brisk steps and a faintly amused expression. When he got close to Buchanan he said, "We must wait five minutes", in a colourless tone.

They both looked at their watches to check the time. Buchanan had an automatic Omega with a calendar, on a flexible stainless steel strap; de Kort's watch was obviously more valuable, in a thin gold case, with elegant Roman numerals, on a black hide strap. They both showed the time to be two forty. De Kort shrugged. "Well, now I know where we are going at least. A bizarre choice for a meeting place in my opinion, but that's up to Harry. Do you know the Amstelkring Museum, 'Our Lord in the Attic'?"

"No. That's where we're meeting?"

"Yes, it's just up the street from here. Two minutes' walk. An interesting, odd place. A clandestine church built into an attic—in fact it extends over three houses, one on the canal here and two smaller houses behind. It was built about 1660 by Jan Hartman when there was an official ban on Catholic worship. Another sign of our tolerance I suppose, or at least a token of liberalism in a generally intolerant age. You see, when the city had gone over to the Calvinist Church the Catholics were allowed to continue holding their services privately, if they were discreet. Not really *clandestine* meetings, because the authorities knew about them and turned a blind eye. On a Monday, out of the main tourist period, you may have the place to yourselves, though occasionally they still hold weddings there. Worth re-visiting some time without Harry, if I may say so. Okay, I've finished my five-minute lecture. Off we go."

They walked in silence along the Oudezijds Voorburgwal where the canal side was lined with parked cars. They were entering the area renowned for brothels, blue films and sex shops. De Kort indicated seedy-looking premises with a waving hand and a disapproving look. "Sometimes I think we're rather too tolerant. A 'living sex-show'—what kind of people take part in that? Oh well ..."

After another minute of silent walking, de Kort stopped. "Here we are. Number 40. Harry said he would be right up at the top. I'll say goodbye now. Don't forget, Buchanan, when

127

you make your sixth trip to Amsterdam telephone me and
we'll have a meal."

"I'd like that very much. Thanks and goodbye."

They shook hands and de Kort strode off, turning once
to call out "Good luck". Buchanan watched him for a few
moments. He had been impressed by de Kort's quiet self-
confidence and good sense. He thought Harry Freedson was
fortunate to have de Kort for a friend.

Buchanan enjoyed entering the Amstelkring Museum; it
was like being given the entrée to one of the fine old
merchants' houses still furnished in seventeenth-century
style. He paid the entrance fee and decided he would come
back on another trip when his mind was not obsessed by the
meeting with Freedson.

With barely a glance at the delightful living-rooms he
ascended the narrow staircase. It seemed as if he were alone
in the place apart from the girl on the ground floor who
sold tickets. Straining his ears to catch any sound from above,
he mentally insured himself against the disappointment of a
possible let-down. After the cloak-and-dagger stuff of the past
half-hour he felt it was still possible that Freedson might not
turn up.

Though Herman de Kort had given him a capsule history
of 'Our Lord in the Attic', Buchanan experienced a feeling
of surprise on reaching the top floor and entering the long
room set out exactly like a Catholic church with rows of
pews, a gallery and an elaborate altar behind which there was
a very large oil-painting. The altar was flanked by two silver
angels but there was no sign of Freedson.

Buchanan had no religious beliefs and he found the atmosphere of the place oppressive. There was a musty smell of
old wood, candle smoke and incense. Standing still, he could
hear what sounded like a whispering noise in the gallery
behind the top of the painting.

As he walked towards some wooden steps by the altar
the whispering sound became urgent, impassioned, more like

whimpering than praying. Buchanan took two steps up and then experienced a sight that shocked him momentarily. He was confronted by what appeared to be a gorilla in man's clothing, holding a gun at a small man's head. The victim was kneeling, holding up an arm as if to ward off the revolver.

The disturbing illusion lasted only for a second. With another step into the darkened area behind the painting Buchanan could see that the larger figure was that of a man with a black woollen helmet pulled over his face so that it made a mask, with small holes cut out for his eyes and mouth. The man in the black woollen mask swung round, shoving the small man to the floor, pointing the revolver at Buchanan's face. Buchanan instinctively lurched first left then right, striking out with his right fist. He landed a solid punch just as the masked man struck out with the hand holding the gun.

Instead of the echoing shot which he had expected Buchanan felt a massive blow on his right shoulder, one that took him off balance so that he fell against the wall. The next moment he found himself on the floor staring across the room as the man in the mask stood still, hesitating. Colliding with the wall had knocked the breath from Buchanan and he could only get up slowly, feeling certain that at any moment he would be shot. But the masked man turned round and climbed out of a window, and instantly disappeared from sight. There was a loud clattering noise.

Buchanan moved to the window and saw that the masked man had made a staggering leap of six or seven feet across to the roof of the next house. It was an awesome jump, one that Buchanan might have attempted in order to save his own life but without any confidence of landing safely. The man on the roof was crouching down in a precarious position, facing away from Buchanan, leaning with his right hand and shoulder against the wet tiles. His back, clothed in a white macintosh, rose and fell for a few moments as he waited to regain his breath. The revolver dropped from his hand, slid down the tiles, bounced on the stone parapet and then spun in a hypnotising slow arc to the alley-way some sixty or seventy feet below. He moved cautiously along the parapet, turned the corner of the roof, and vanished.

Buchanan heard a muffled noise behind him and looked round to see that the small man was kneeling and retching. His thin black hair had fallen forward revealing a bald crown. He retched loudly again but was not sick. He was chalk-white and sweating. He brushed his face with both hands, swallowed and said: "Christ, I was the lucky one there all right! You're Buchanan?"

"Yes."

"What did that maniac do then?"

"He jumped. A fantastic jump!"

"Well come on for fuck's sake. Let's get out of here."

XIX

WHEN Freedson and Buchanan left the Amstelkring Museum they did so in as calm a fashion as they could manage. They had run down a different set of stairs, led by Freedson who obviously knew every passage and stairway in the rabbit-warren made by connecting three houses together. All the time they could hear excited voices, and a woman shouting incoherent instructions. When they reached the ground floor Freedson stopped for a moment to push back his dishevelled hair, roughly dusted his trousers and stepped into the entrance hall, making some banal remark about a silver sanctuary lamp.

Buchanan took Freedson's cue and said, "Oh yes", then realised that the girl who took the tickets had left her post, and their little charade had been superfluous. They went out into the street and found that there was a crowd of people staring up at the roof. An American in a brown gaberdine suit kept repeating: "What is it, Joanie? What is it? Joanie, what did you see?" An old Dutchman pointed vaguely upwards and said something in a heavily accented, cawing voice that Buchanan could not understand at all. Freedson stood still as if only mildly interested by the odd incident which had attracted so many pedestrians.

"Wat gebeurde er?"

"Viel er iemand?"

"Ik denk een ongeluk."

"Ik zag een man weghollen."

"Der politie komt er aan."

Hearing this last sentence Freedson nodded sagely and said: "Yes, it's all right. It seems the police *are* coming. But there's nothing to see so we might as well go." They began to walk slowly along the Oudezijds Voorburgwal in the Zeedijk direction. Once out of earshot of the crowd, Freedson said: "Thanks. We'll talk in a minute. There are some bars and cafés up ahead and we'll pop into one. But thanks."

A plump prostitute was leaning out of an upstairs window trying to make out what was going on outside No. 40. A more attractive one cut across their path, leaving a faint seductive perfume and whispering something indistinct. Freedson smiled. *"Kom naar binnen* indeed! Some chance! She must like your style. In fact I rather like the way you move myself. Jesus! Sid Chard told me that he once knew someone who would go through a brick wall for a box of matches. Now I've met one."

Buchanan shivered. He felt empty and cold. Faced by the revolver, he had moved instinctively. Now there was a reaction at having come so close to death.

They made their way through twisting little streets close to the waterfront where Buchanan caught glimpses of grey wharves and old rotting timbers. Freedson paused by a bold sign offering SEVEN COLOUR TATTOOING—4000 DESIGNS—NO PAIN—NO SCAR and then Buchanan followed him down some steps to a small basement bar.

Buchanan sat at a table in a corner and took off his damp jacket. Freedson came over from the counter carrying two glasses and a bottle of gin. "Is this all right?"

Buchanan nodded. "You bet."

Freedson said quietly: "What the fuck happened? There I was not moving out of my brother's flat for ten days. I leave it for just ten minutes and—crash!"

"He must have been watching the flat."

"But who—and how did he know about the flat?"

"Look, I don't know anything. You told Bee that you had something to give her. I came here just to pick it up. That's all I know. Tell me what's been going on and then I might be able to say something sensible."

Freedson filled the small glasses with gin, then gestured his surprise. "So ... Bee doesn't know anything. Leo didn't tell her ... I thought he might have done. Sid—well, I suppose it's different with Sid and Nora. She's in the business and she's tough. At least I used to think so. Now I don't know. She seems to be too frightened to talk to me."

Buchanan said: "Well I want to talk to you. What is it you're going to give me, and if you're carrying it on you why couldn't you post it?"

Freedson pulled up the edge of one trouser-leg disclosing a thin hairy leg with a large plaster stuck across the calf. He undid one end of the plaster and produced a manilla envelope which had been folded up into a tiny packet. From the envelope he extracted a key.

Buchanan said dully: "You got me here for that?" His hand instinctively touched his sore shoulder.

"The explanation of why I have to get rid of this now is the important part. I've got to explain what I'm doing to Bee and Nora. They wouldn't come here. It's not something I could say over the phone. And I'm certainly not going back there for the time being. My brother lives here, I've got some good friends here too. I could move around for months without surfacing, if necessary."

"Why did you leave London?"

"I'm going to tell you everything. I want to have it all out in the open and then perhaps that masked maniac will go away. At least I hope so. Bee should know what's been going on. Didn't she suspect it might have something to do with that Trewartha sale?"

"No—but Manny Klein had his suspicions."

"Ah, Manny—the cunning old sod. Well, it doesn't matter who knows now. Manny probably told you that Sid, Leo and I bought all the good stuff at the Trewartha sale. Nothing spectacular—we weren't going to make a fortune, and some of the lots were a bit damaged by water. But it was a good day's work. We'd done well. We went out for a meal together once the sale was finished. Sid had fixed it with a porter so that we could come back afterwards, go over the stuff again and hold our own little auction. Sid and Leo were both taken by a lady's rosewood and inlaid writing desk. By Christ, I wish they hadn't been! It has a part cylinder front that works in conjunction with a frieze drawer. Sid fiddled about with it and found out that when the cylinder front was held at a certain point you could pull the frieze drawer out further. There was a small secret drawer at the back. In it Sid found an old notebook that had belonged to that madman Trewartha. Did you know Trewartha went right off his head in the end, lived like a hermit for the last ten years of his life? No, it's no good, I must have something to eat. I was all nerves this morning, couldn't eat at all. Now I feel empty, quite weak. Have something with me?"

"Yes, thanks. I could eat some bread and cheese."

After a few minutes Freedson brought back a large plate covered with slices of black bread, Gouda cheese, liver sausage and ham. He slumped down in the chair and lifted one hand in the air to demonstrate how much it trembled. "You see." Then he made a thick sandwich of sausage and ham, and munched solidly without a word.

When the sandwich was finished he poured himself some

133

more gin. "So we all looked through the notebook. Trewartha had been one of a group of secret fascists before the war, the high-up kind who didn't join the blackshirts or give their hand away at all, but were quite willing to see Hitler conquer Europe and come to some arrangement with him. Powerful men, all of them, a British fifth column in fact. The kind who in France gave orders for divisions to surrender without them firing a shot. Important people. You'd be surprised. Generals, M.P.s."

"General Everard, Lord Gleneale, Henry Cuyp," Buchanan suggested.

Freedson's scanty eyebrows shot up and he pointed significantly with one finger at his head. His gestures had the eloquence of deaf-and-dumb language. "Where the hell did you get those names?"

"I didn't get them out of a hat. Leo wrote them down, with several others, under the heading *Eendracht Maakt Macht!*"

"Did he, by God! He must have copied that out of the notebook. It was a list of key members of the group. 'Unity makes strength.' It could have done too. Imagine if Hitler had invaded Britain what effect a group like that could have had. But what a stupid thing for Leo to do! You see, we were all out of our depth, fooling around with real danger. Why the hell did we do it? I blame Sid. Yes, all of it down to Sid. He can be very persuasive, you know. Anyway, that's my excuse. Sid talked us into it."

"Into what?"

"Sid said we shouldn't include the desk in the knockout, said we'd all have an equal share in the desk and its contents, that we should meet at his flat and discuss what to do with it at our leisure. So that's what we did. We met at Sid's flat a week later when he'd had the furniture brought up in a van. By that time he'd come up with this mad idea. He'd been looking into things, found out that a lot of the men on the list were dead. But three were probably alive and one certainly was, alive and extremely prosperous. A merchant banker named Henry Cuyp, Managing Director of the Arkadie Company, now living in Eaton Square. So Sid said we should offer to sell him the desk and the contents intact."

"Blackmail. Chard must have known that was a possible charge that could be brought."

"Sid was sure he could handle it. You've never met him, have you? He's not as strong as you but he's got just as much nerve. For a while we thought he had pulled it off. He went to see Cuyp, took along some photostats of pages in the notebook, and offered to let Cuyp have the desk complete with contents for £50,000. Cuyp didn't get excited about it. Sid said that Cuyp seemed to regard it as an unfortunate business but nothing more dramatic—said he would have to contact some friends and let Sid know. By that time we'd found out that General Sir Claude Everard was definitely alive too. Very interesting about Everard. You see, he had a big job in the Army in 1939 but lost it in 1940, so perhaps someone somewhere had suspicions about him. Now he's living in South Africa, owns a great estate there. He's probably as wealthy as Cuyp. Like Sid said, £50,000 wouldn't seem a great sum to men like that."

"Did you get it?"

"Not a sausage. Fact is, old Sid had met his match in Henry Cuyp. He would never admit it but that's the truth. Cuyp kept on promising that he would keep to his side of the bargain if he was given enough time, and Sid believed him. Of course he's a mighty smooth and shrewd character, Henry Cuyp. Everything he said was reasonable. That others were involved and they would have to help him find the money. Eventually he said that Everard was coming to the U.K. in August and the business would be settled then. So Sid agreed. I mean, he might threaten to send the notebook to a newspaper, but what satisfaction would he get out of that when there was even a remote chance of getting the cash? The funny thing is we all reacted differently to that notebook. I just thought 'What's in

135

it for me?' and 'Can Sid finagle it?' Whereas for Sid it was also some kind of revenge for his being buggered about by the Nazis during the war. He got his knee smashed somewhere in Italy you see. There's a lot of suppressed aggression in Sid. You wind him up and off he goes."

"What about Leo? It's out of character for him. At least I should have thought so."

"You're right. Poor old Leo. He didn't like it much. But he'd become a rather cynical character you know, always wondering what life was all about. He was the only one of us who was really interested in that notebook, kept poring over it. Part of it was in a simple code. Leo made sense of most of it eventually. It seemed to make a much bigger impact on him—the mystery about that madman Trewartha, the plot, all the men who had been in it, who the 'Court-Card' on the list was. Sid and I didn't care about all that. We were just interested in the idea of some tax-free cash."

"What do you think happened to Sid?"

"No idea. We knew he was waiting for a call from Cuyp. Then suddenly he vanished. And with Leo dying more or less the same day, it was too much of a coincidence for me. I know Leo died of a heart attack but he couldn't have killed the girl. Not a chance! So with Sid and Leo both gone— just as if somebody had leant down and taken two pawns off a chess-table—I wasn't going to wait around for other moves of the same kind. So I came here. The thing about today is that I tried to be too crafty. I didn't want to give you my brother's address, yet I wanted to meet you somewhere out of the way. So that was my mistake. But the man in the mask made one as well. There was too much menace! If he had just come up to me behind the altar and hit me once with his fist as hard as he hit you, he could have had the key. But that mask and the gun—I was so scared I couldn't get a word out or think straight. Talk about a steam-roller to break a nut!"

"You've no idea who he could be?"

"Someone hired by Cuyp—well I suppose that's most likely. But Sid didn't figure he would do anything like that. I don't know. All I want now is to be finished with it."

"You've put me in an awkward position."

"You mean about going to the police? Forget it. I know the police will have to come into it. Nora seems to think that by doing nothing everything unpleasant will go away. But she's got to face up to it. The police will have to make inquiries. I doubt if they'll bring charges against me. First of all, they've got to have Cuyp as a witness to a charge of blackmail. No jury is ever going to convict me on your story about what I told you in a bar in Smids Steeg. No, you go ahead, tell Bee and Nora what happened. Tell Nora she must go to the police. It's going to be an unhappy ending for Nora as well as for Bee I'm afraid. Something really bad must have happened to Sid. I scare myself stiff just thinking about it."

"Right. I'll do that. And the key?"

"The key opens a Post Box in the G.P.O. in Rathbone Place. That's a turning off Oxford Street. You'll find the note-book there. Division of labour, you see. Poor Leo puzzled out the code in the book, Sid went to see Henry Cuyp, and I held on to our ace in the hole. What a mess! The joke of it is that none of us was hard up or needed the money really badly. Just greedy at the chance of tax-free loot. Tell Bee and Nora I'm sorry—say I regret every day—no, just tell them I'm sorry."

XX

MAKING a phone-call to Nora Chard from the London Air Terminal was a disconcerting experience for Ed Buchanan. Even at the start her voice was uncertain, and there was a continuous background noise of a television or radio programme with bursts of laughter and applause. He explained that he had to see her, saying that he was a friend of Beatrice Selver and had been to Amsterdam to talk to Harry Freedson. At the mention of Freedson's name Mrs. Chard dropped the receiver. When she spoke again her phrases were disjointed: "What does Harry want? Is it Sid? I can't bear ... Don't say ..."

Buchanan tried to explain that he had no direct news about Sidney Chard, only an important message from Freedson, but it seemed as if Mrs. Chard was unable to accept this. Her reply was even more rambling and Buchanan wondered whether she was becoming hysterical. She must have been hiding her fears for so long that she had now reached breaking point. He tried to calm her down with vague reassurances. Suddenly the incoherent sentences stopped. She agreed to see him at two o'clock and replaced the receiver.

In a bus on his way to Oxford Street Buchanan said mentally: "Let's warm up the ice-cubes". He knew that he was going to need a drink or two before meeting Mrs. Chard. No matter how he tried, he would be unable to rake up any good news for her: the facts were simply that her husband had been involved in an attempt to extort a considerable sum of money through blackmail; that one of his conspirators had died in strange circumstances, and the other one had gone abroad and was too frightened to leave his hiding-place. Unless Nora Chard had definite information about her husband's present whereabouts his disappearance must be considered an ominous matter. There was no need to tell her of the bizarre masked figure that had terrorised Freedson behind the altar painting, but she must be persuaded to be frank with the police.

Buchanan walked along Rathbone Place, entered the large Post Office building there and, following Freedson's instructions, opened the Postal Box. It contained one stout-looking envelope sealed with Sellotape. He placed it inside his windcheater jacket and walked out swinging the BOAC bag which

Katie had lent him for the trip to Amsterdam. A sensation of guilt at now being involved with the blackmail plot, even though quite innocently, made him feel that a postman might come up and query his right to have opened the box.

This feeling persisted all the way along Rathbone Place and as he crossed over Percy Street, gradually changing to the equally illogical belief that now he had the vital notebook in his possession he too might be followed. In Charlotte Street he stood outside an Italian restaurant pretending to study the menu but glancing back along his path. The belief that he was under observation was absurd but he found it hard to dismiss. He knew he was now in the area where Leo Selver had died—only a few hundred feet in fact from the house in Stephen Street awaiting demolition. Phrases from the press-report of the double death came into his mind. He remembered the comments of Judy Latimer's neighbours: "We hardly knew her ... She seemed pleasant but rarely said anything more than 'Good morning' ... We didn't even know her first name ..."

When Buchanan's parents had both been killed in a car crash he had found it difficult to accept the fact of their extinction for some weeks: during that period there had been occasions when he believed that it might have been a bad dream. It seemed equally improbable that only a month previously Leo Selver had been walking along these streets, possibly turning the very same corner, and now was a refrigerated corpse.

Buchanan entered the Yorkshire Grey pub in Maple Street where there was a pleasant atmosphere in which he could relax and have a snack while glancing at the notebook. He ordered a Guinness, some bread and cheese and a slice of pork-pie.

"After you with the mustard, laddie." The man saying this as he leant across Buchanan looked as if he had done a lot of work in his time with a knife and fork. The word "laddie", spoken in a mock old actor's timbre, echoed and lingered

139

in Buchanan's mind. It evoked his strange conversation with "Mr. Quentin", and something in that faked voice reminded him in turn of another one that he had heard in the past few days. But the idea was vague and tantalising, hovering just out of reach round a bend in his mind as did any interpretation of his intuition over the talk with Toby Crest.

He took his plate and the glass of Guinness to a table. When he had finished the food he opened the heavy linen envelope and pulled out a small notebook bound in green leather that was worn and crumbling at the corners. About a dozen small pieces of ruled paper had been inserted, presumably to mark pages of particular interest, but Buchanan began at the start of the book. The opening pages were taken up with a few rambling notes, written in faded green ink, about the iniquities of international Jewry, the hold that Jews had on finance and politics, "the necessity of fighting a Jewish octopus now threatening England—a threat of similar magnitude to that of red domination".

The first narrow slip of paper marked the page in the notebook where there was the list of names headed *"Eendracht maakt Macht"*. Most of the other pages indicated by slips were written in code. The cipher consisted of blocks of letters without any breaks. On one slip there was a note in pencil. "N.B. Conversation in May, 1940, between Lord Trewartha, General Sir Claude Everard and Brigadier Fitzroy in which they discussed a list of officers in Home Command whose views on the war situation were to be sounded out with regard to possible peace negotiations." Another note was written in red ink with the first two words heavily underlined. "Trewartha's cellar. Cellar in the kitchen made into a secret strong-room. Trewartha's possession of a transceiver kept in the cellar."

Trewartha's cellar and its secret contents were noted again on other slips, and there was a transcription in part of a later conversation between Trewartha, Everard, Cuyp and Fitzroy, with the brief underlined comment in red "Treason".

Buchanan could understand the fascination that the notebook had for Leo Selver: it would have been easy to spend an hour poring over its secrets which had been hidden away for thirty-three years, but he had an appointment with Mrs. Chard and he did not intend to keep her waiting.

Walking along Charlotte Street again Buchanan heard the sound of recorded *bouzouki* music coming from a Greek restaurant, and it immediately evoked memories of clear blue skies above Samos, the distant wail of a *klephtic* song, sun beating down on deserted beaches, and waking up in the night to the endless quiet washing sound of the sea. He stopped to look up at the dirty grey sky covering London: it was rapidly darkening and there was a distinct promise of rain before long. As he hurried towards Tottenham Court Road he knew that the events of the past few days had at least got rid of his desire to find a way of life like that on Samos. He was going to make a real effort to settle down in England, even if it meant going back to work for Bathwick Mews Performance Cars.

Bedford Place Mansions was situated within sight of the British Museum, a pleasant-looking block of flats constructed of dark red brick, probably sixty or seventy years old. The lift looked as if it might be the original one with its double wrought-iron gates: it grumbled and took its time going up two floors, coming to a halt with a shudder.

The door of the Chard's flat was opened by a large formidable-looking woman with dyed blonde hair the improbable colour of canary feathers. Her large grey eyes were uncomfortably alert and suspicious. As Buchanan introduced himself her face was held in a taut, faintly scornful expression. She nodded several times and made an ineffectual little gesture.

"Yes, yes, come in." Turning to lead the way, she parted an invisible curtain with her hands and appeared to shiver. As they entered a large living-room she looked round into Buchanan's face, saying: "I'm sorry. I'm not well." Her breath smelt of brandy masked by toothpaste. She had made a sketchy attempt at make-up but the bright orange lipstick and two streaks of green eye-shadow only emphasised her unhealthy pallor.

Buchanan was no judge of furniture but even to his eye the pieces that filled the room were quite impressive. A cowboy film was being shown on the television screen. Nora Chard turned down the sound but left the picture on.

"So Harry hasn't seen Sid at all?"

"Not in the last month. You've no idea where he might be?"

"I was hoping ... There was a chance I thought ... You see Sid knows Harry's brother who lives in Amsterdam. Oh God, what am I going to do?"

"What did your husband say? When he went away."

"On the Tuesday, that was the 14th of August—that afternoon he said he would be setting off early in the morning, taking his car. Wanted to have breakfast about seven and leave at half seven. Said he didn't know exactly when he would be back. Took an overnight bag with just a few things. He often did that. I was used to it. He seemed to be rather cagey—strange with me—but I thought, let it go. When he didn't come back—two days afterwards—I went to the garage where he keeps his car, just round the corner in Gower Street. They said yes, he'd had the oil and tyres checked and the tank filled early on the Wednesday morning and had driven off."

"The tank filled. What kind of car is it?"

"A Rover 3500. The sort that some of the police have."

"Oh yes, I know. The tank holds fifteen gallons. Do you think he was going on a long journey?"

"He might have been, at least he was keyed up like he often was before a long-distance trip. His leg bothers him sometimes driving."

"And you haven't heard anything since then?"

"Nothing that makes any sense. Harry Freedson keeps on

talking about some deal having fallen through, wanting me to go out there and see him. As if he was frightened to say what he really meant. Of course that's just scared me all the more."

"And you haven't been to the police?"

"No. I know I should have—I've been frightened ..."

"Yes, I understand. But you'll have to see them. I know somebody who'd come round here and have a talk with you. A nice chap." Saying this, Buchanan could not help feeling irritated that Machin had dismissed the tip about Chard with "Some pieces belong t'noother jigsaw altogether".

"Sid got mixed up in something dodgy, didn't he? I knew it. There were some phone-calls ..."

"Yes, he did—with Leo and Harry. But whatever the police may do about that is quite unimportant compared to tracing your husband, Mrs. Chard. You mustn't leave it any longer."

Nora Chard groaned and put her face in her hands. Her heavy body shook as if she was sobbing but there were no tears. She seemed to want to cry but was incapable of obtaining this relief. She made another groaning noise.

"What's wrong, mummy?" The door had been opened quietly by a small boy, about ten or eleven years old, thin and pale, with dark hair. He looked accusingly at Buchanan from behind thick glasses.

Buchanan said: "Your mum's upset. She's had some bad news. Would you like a drink, Mrs. Chard? Shall I make you some coffee?"

"No, thank you. Perhaps—a glass of water."

Buchanan went into the hall and found that a door opposite was open, leading into a bathroom fitted out in a dated luxurious style. The walls were covered with pale green tiles with an art nouveau design, and the hand-basin had marble surrounds. A marble-topped table was covered with jars and bottles. The basin had old-fashioned heavy brass taps. As he was filling a tumbler he heard someone behind him and turned to find the small boy staring up with a look of strain as though he had to correct a distorted vision.

"Mummy says she would like some tea, not water. She didn't have any lunch. I can make the tea."

Buchanan nodded, saying: "That's good. What's your name? Mine's Ed. I'm a friend of Mrs. Selver—I expect you know her."

"Clive. Do you know what's happened to my dad?"

"No, I don't, but I hope we can find out something soon. Your mum's going to ask the police to help now."

Buchanan followed the boy into the hall and then into the kitchen, saying: "As your mum's upset it would be a good idea if you could get one of her friends to pop round for a while. Do you know someone?"

"My Auntie Joyce. That's mummy's sister. She lives in Earl's Court."

"You suggest that, Clive. I'm going to make some inquiries about your dad myself. What colour is the car?"

"It's dark green. A Rover V8 automatic. MUX 121K."

"Good boy. I'll write the number down. Try and help your mum all you can. And be careful with that kettle. So long Clive. I expect I'll see you again soon."

Buchanan looked into the living-room to find that Nora Chard had switched off the television and pulled the curtain behind it, which had made the room dark. She was standing looking out of the window. "I'm all right now—feel a bit better."

"I was just saying to young Clive that you ought to get a friend round. Someone you can talk to. You've been bottling everything up too long. I've got to go now but I'll phone tomorrow in case there's any news. And I'll tell Inspector Machin to call. Okay?"

"Yes—and thanks." Nora Chard put out a large capable-looking hand. She was a woman who had been used to making decisions, working hard to help her husband build up a business while running her home. Suddenly she had been faced by a situation that must have swept away all the satis-

144

factions of a successful career, one that had made her groan. Even so she had her chin up and was preparing herself to face whatever the future had in store. She had none of Beatrice Selver's charm, nor her feminine appeal to male protectiveness, but Buchanan left the flat with a strong desire to help her if he could.

XXI

ED BUCHANAN drove from West London to the edge of Bodmin Moor in just over four hours, with a break for eggs and bacon and tea at a café on the A30. He had caught a bus for Paddington on an impulse after leaving the Chard's flat, walked to Bathwick Mews and asked Ken Hughes if he could borrow a car till the following morning. Hughes had offered him the choice of four and Buchanan picked a 1970 De Tomaso Mangusta, which was in good nick with only 20,000 miles on the clock and brand-new Pirelli tyres.

The idea that Sidney Chard might have set off for Trewartha Place on that morning in August, when he had made an early start in his Rover with a full tank of petrol, was one that Buchanan felt he had to test. There would be no satisfaction if he were to discover Chard's corpse in the much-written-about cellar of the moorland house, but the quest had a strong fascination. From Hughes he had also borrowed a large torch cased in black rubber, a coil of stout rope, a tyre-lever, a plastic mac, and sheet 186 of the Ordnance Survey maps, which covered the Bodmin Moor area.

Waiting for his eggs and bacon to be cooked, he had flicked through Trewartha's notebook again. One of the slips bore a note in Leo Selver's hand: "Playfair cipher. This passage relates to treason and quotes 'an ancient statute of Edward III of 1351: Or if a man do levy war against our Lord the King in his realm, or be adherent to the enemies of our Lord

145

the King in the realm, bringing to them aid and comfort in his realm, or elsewhere ...' "

After glancing at some other passages which did not seem to be of great significance, he turned to a closer study of the Ordnance Survey map. A minor road ran past Twelve Men's Moor and Trewartha Tor, then a track continued to a place named as King Arthur's Bed, where two streams met in an area shown to be marshy. After a marked building which he took to be Trewartha Place there was no sign of the track continuing. The house appeared to be isolated in the very heart of the moor, surrounded only by hills and marshland.

Driving along the A30 after the Exeter bypass, Buchanan was struck by the disconcerting idea that he was being followed by someone in a cherry-red Volkswagen. The Mangusta had plenty of acceleration and several times he passed a bunch of slow-moving cars, only to spot the Volkswagen again in his driving mirror.

He realised that the driver of the Volkswagen might just be pitting himself against the exotic-looking Mangusta, but did not like the other possibility that he was being followed, and was happier when the red car turned left off the A30 just past Okehampton. Once the Volkswagen had gone Buchanan was able to enjoy putting the Swiss car through its paces: it was years since he had driven a car responsive to sensitive handling.

From Launceston his route was via South Petherwin and the oddly named Congdon's Shop. He made good time to the very edge of the moor and then promptly got lost in a maze of small lanes where there were no signposts, or houses where he could inquire about directions. Though it was only 8 p.m. the sky was quite dark with storm-clouds, and he found it necessary to drive on dipped headlights. After wasting ten minutes during which he crossed the River Lynher twice he heard the sound of a tractor. He got out of the car, picked up his map and ran along a muddy lane. The driver of the tractor, who was manoeuvring a loaded truck out of a field, stared down at him suspiciously.

"Sorry to bother you but I'm lost. I'm trying to get to Trewartha Place. Sounds stupid, but I can't work out where I am on the map."

The tractor-driver nodded slowly, switching off his engine and looking Buchanan up and down. "'Tis a brave walk."

"No, I'm not walking. I've got a car parked just round the corner."

The driver got down from the tractor, saying nothing but pulling on his nose with a doubtful expression. He stared hard for a few moments and then pointed a grimy finger at Buchanan as if making an accusation. "Well, you won't get there apart from one track and don't you go off that for no reason! Not two years since the Army thought they knew better'n us about such things, and blowed if they didn't lose a tank along there. More luck than judgment they didn't lose the lads in the tank too. You mind what I say 'cos there's quaking bog near Rushyford Gate and by Withy Brook."

"You show me the way on the map and I'll stick to the track all right."

"I don't know that I shouldn't advise you 'gainst it. 'Tis nothing to see but an old house burnt down. Still I 'spect you know your own business best."

The man in the green denim overalls took the map and scratched its surface with a horny-looking nail. "You're just here at Nodmans Bowda. Why I said afore about getting there but by the one track as there's another marked there, see! But you'd find it peters out afore you get to Twelve Men's Moor. No, your only road is go right back and turn left just afore Berriowbridge. Then bear left all the way. Take it slowly now and that track 'twill be all right. It was safe enough for those fire-engines and removal vans. But go off it and that's that." He dismissed the hope of survival in that event with a wave of his hand. "You mind now!"

Walking back to the white Mangusta Buchanan became aware of how strong the wind was, whipping the tops of trees this way and that, and driving the rain horizontally into his face. The car's cobalt headlights gave a curious dead look to the dripping trees and bushes. He could not remember driving anywhere else in England where there were no signs of human life. Sticking to his directions and travelling at a slower pace than the Mangusta liked, he soon reached a hilly area and for the first time saw the bleak face of the moor itself, where wind and rain had eroded the soil, littering the higher slopes with granite boulders.

After driving for ten minutes he came to the end of the tarred road where there was a white gate and a notice: STRICTLY PRIVATE—TREWARTHA PLACE ONLY—TRESPASSERS WILL BE PROSECUTED. As he undid the gate he could see that the tractor-driver had not exaggerated the possible danger in driving along the track, for there was a stream running alongside on the left and to the right a marshy area with waterlogged hollows and moss-covered hummocks stretching as far as he could see. There was no doubt that he had made a mistake in choosing the Mangusta for this trip; it was like a spirited race-horse, great for covering ground on a motorway, but at its worst being driven slowly along a peaty track with a thin covering of heather.

It would have been prudent to leave the car at the white gate but Buchanan had not reached the age of prudence. In the distance he could see the large stone house that was his goal, and it had an urgent allure for him. After another few minutes he had reached the heavy iron gates before the house and had parked the Mangusta there.

Trewartha Place stood on rising ground and behind it there were hills that looked black and mysterious in the fading light. A few trees silhouetted on the slopes were all forced over in one direction by the prevailing south-west winds. Buchanan ran his hand over a much eroded coat of arms on the gate's stone pillar, like a blind man reading braille. He could just trace the outline of a rampant lion.

The stone façade of the house was intact but there were

no windows and the sky was visible through one of the broken frames, showing that part of the back wall must have gone. Buchanan picked up the torch, tyre-lever and rope. He knew that he must watch himself in getting down into the cellar: if he had an accident no one would be around to help him, but the spice of danger was something he needed from time to time. As he made his way through a tangle of brambles and giant weeds to the ruined house he felt a surge of excitement and a heightened sense of life. The cold wind blowing over the bleak moorland was like a disintegrating force, a chilly breath from the void. He enjoyed tackling a tricky task when circumstances seemed to conspire against him.

The front wall of the house acted like a mask to conceal the havoc immediately behind it—there were piles of charred beams and stone rubble, splintered floorboards and window-frames. He picked his way with some care: after coming so far he did not want to tread on a nail and then be out of the game. Looking round he could see that an attempt had been made to bring some kind of order to the ruined property, presumably by the firemen in their search for Trewartha's body. A stone staircase, suitable for a pantomime finale, was intact but nearly all of the second floor of the house had collapsed. A lavatory cistern still clung to one upstairs wall though the basin had fallen and smashed. A bath stood upright, full of water.

The wind whined through the window spaces and holes in the walls, making a dismal sobbing sound. Buchanan clambered over a pile of smashed and blackened furniture to the rear of the house where he could see an old-fashioned stove in one corner. He dropped the rope and tyre-lever on the stove and manhandled chunks of stone and wood from the kitchen floor. Half-way through this task he spotted a wooden cover in a space already cleared; a broken padlock lay close by it. He tugged at an iron handle set into the cover and it opened easily with a whiff of an old crypt-like atmosphere. With his torch he looked down a flight of slime-

149

covered stone steps. He laid the cover right back and went down the slippery steps cautiously.

The cellar was on two levels, and on the first one there were some steel filing-cabinets sealed with rust. An orgy of destruction had taken place there at some time as the floor was covered with torn-up papers, files ripped in half, and boxes smashed to matchwood. A hammer had been used to dent great holes in the cabinets. Buchanan picked up what appeared to be part of a German book and studied one page. The printed text consisted of a list of numbers and addresses:

53. Weizmann, Chaim, 1873 oder 1874 in Motyli bei Pinks, Professor der Chemie, Führer der gesamten Juden-vereine Englands, London S.W.1, 104 Pall Mall, Reform-Club, RSHA II B 2, VI G 1.

54. Welker, Helene, 13.12.04 Berlin RSHA IV A 2.

55. Wells, Herbert George, 1866 geb. Schriftsteller, London, N.W.1, Regents Park 13, Hanover Terrace, RSHA VI G 1, III A 5 II B 4.

55a. Welsh, brit. N.-Agent, zuletzi: Kopenhagen, vermut 1. England, RSHA IV E 4.

Buchanan pocketed this odd relic of Lord Trewartha's secret life as a traitor and shone his powerful torch on the second level of the cellar. There were four more steps down to the glistening black water. Fragments of broken wine-racks and scraps of paper floated on its surface. The smell of stagnant slime was strong and repugnant, but Buchanan shone his torch and scrutinised every inch. Someone had discovered the cellar door and removed the padlock. Had it been a curious fireman, or perhaps Sidney Chard in search of other evidence of Trewartha's treacherous activities?

"Ah, Mr. Buchanan!" The commonplace greeting boomed and echoed in Buchanan's ears with a more sinister significance than any threat. He swung his torch round to show Richard

Madoc standing on the first flight of the steps, holding a torch in one hand and a large automatic in the other.

Madoc flicked on his own torch and said: "I'll take the notebook."

"And then bury me here like you did Chard?" Buchanan indicated the stagnant water.

"Don't be a fool. That water's not a foot deep. No one's buried there. Some broken bottles perhaps."

Buchanan stared at Madoc's expressionless face that was like a handsome mask and the glittering dark eyes that hinted at a psychotic drive. He was puzzled that Madoc had not already used the gun to take the notebook. He said: "Oh yes, you buried Chard here somewhere. And you had a hand in Leo Selver's death too. I don't know how but I'm sure of it. You've got a Chinese girl working for you. I remember that now. She was seen with Judy Latimer."

Madoc said: "Come on. Hand over the notebook. Stop scaring yourself with all this rubbish. I've as much right to the book as you, and I'm going to have it." He raised the automatic so that the barrel pointed straight at Buchanan's throat. "One way or the other."

Buchanan had a sensitive ear that could detect a faint ring of perplexity or doubt in a voice. Now his belief was that Madoc's threats, even though backed up by a Luger, were not as firm as they should be. Madoc seemed to be bluffing. Buchanan had been close to death several times in his motor-racing career, and faced by Madoc's gun he did not feel that stomach-churning knowledge; he sensed that, strange as it seemed, there was fear in Madoc's voice. He said: "Yes, you buried Chard somewhere here. You were 'Mr. Quentin' too, tried to have me put out of the way. Perhaps I'd better ..." With his left hand he fumbled with his jacket zip as if reaching inside and then hurled his torch at Madoc's chest. A moment later he leapt forward expecting to hear the boom of the Luger, but instead grappling with Madoc as he fell down the steps.

In a moment they were wrestling with each other in the dark among the rubbish. The only light came in weird flashes as Madoc tried to use his torch like a club. Madoc was shouting out "Now you see" and "This time" like a maniac. Buchanan took some hard blows on the shoulders but concentrated on tearing the Luger from Madoc's right hand and throwing it backwards into the water. Then he brought his knee up into Madoc's groin. He did this with all his strength and the savage blow made Madoc scream out. Madoc's ravings changed into sobs and groans. Buchanan punched away solidly with his right fist as he tried to hold off the torch with his left. Madoc yelped with pain and swung the torch round wildly in an arc penetrating Buchanan's defence, laying open a cut across his forehead so that blood poured down into his eyes. Another blow hit him on the side of the head and he blacked out.

After falling into darkness for what seemed like a few seconds he realised he was alone in the cellar. The only light was the one he could see dimly through the entrance. He brushed his face with his sleeve to clear the blood from his eyes and scrambled up the steps. When he came out into the cold rain it cleared his head. He caught sight of Madoc running away as fast as he could, still shouting out wild threats to the night sky.

Buchanan's legs felt numb but he forced himself to chase after Madoc who had nearly reached the iron gates. The impulse to follow was the illogical and primitive one of revenge. His face was covered in blood and he could taste it continuously. He kept on thinking: I'll make him pay. He had no plans other than to stop Madoc.

When Buchanan stepped warily round the iron gates he saw that Madoc was already seated behind the wheel in the cherry-red Volkswagen which had followed the Mangusta along the A30. The driver's door of the car was still wide open but Madoc had started the engine; he was moving about in the front seats like a lunatic, holding his head and shout-

152

ing something incomprehensible. Suddenly the small car leapt straight at Buchanan, who waited a moment and then threw himself sideways towards the stone wall, banging his right shoulder hard against the ancient pillar which bore the Trewartha coat of arms.

Madoc must have driven with his foot right down on the accelerator because the car shot across the small patch of grass in front of the gates and off the track as if it were taking flight. It landed in the desolate area of bog and Buchanan heard a soft thud and chilling screams. He raced down to the edge of the track shouting: "Get out, you clown! For Christ's sake get out!"

He reached the end of the Volkswagen's tracks in the wet rank grass in a few seconds but already the car had sunk in the bog above its wheels and liquid mud was pouring in through the open door. Madoc seemed to be wrestling with something unseen as if trapped by an invisible hazard and unable to leave the sinking car. Buchanan called out again to him, looking around desperately. The Volkswagen was some twenty feet out from the track. He sat down on the edge of the bank and lowered his feet into the bog, trying to find a part that would take his weight. His feet sank wherever he put them and it took all his strength to pull them out. He saw a hummock of sphagnum moss about four feet away and turned on to his side to reach it, but it broke under the pressure of his foot and was immediately covered in water.

Madoc was drowning in the liquid mud. His contorted face, as if frozen in a silent scream and covered in black muck, was visible at the top of the open door for a few moments, and then sank out of sight.

The car was vanishing with a ghastly sucking noise. Buchanan was as close to a feeling of panic as he had ever been in his life. The frustration of not being able to do anything to help was practically unbearable but he knew that if he entered the bog he would drown too. His mind was

153

jumbling up terror and pity, and the violence of his emotion was such that he was hardly conscious of what he was doing. The last image of the top of the red car covered by an ever thickening veil of muddy water was a loathsome one. With tears in his eyes he ran back to the ruined house to fetch the coil of rope. He knew that any action towards saving Madoc was doomed but he had to do something, no matter how futile.

XXII

ON a perfect autumn day, in the last week of October 1973, Ed Buchanan walked along the Mall and turned into St. James's Park. The park was in ambling distance for Detective Chief Superintendent Jack Collier who would be coming from the New Scotland Yard building in the Broadway at Victoria. It was a good public place for a strictly private meeting. Buchanan did not plan to do any shouting but he wanted to speak his mind, preferably in a place where he could not be overheard or recorded on tape.

It was eleven a.m. The morning mist had cleared and been replaced by hazy sunshine but the air was still crisp and seemed to generate energy. Buchanan strolled along a path in the park with a strong awareness of the physical world about him and pleasure in its appearance. He enjoyed the sunlight flashing on the lake and seagulls circling above it, the faint sounds of a military band, the perfume stealing from a bed of tobacco plants and stocks, the bright colours of the dahlias. Everything about London seemed to be contrived for pleasure. His life was taking shape at last and making sense. Being treated as a prospective partner by Ken Hughes had made a lot of difference to working at the Bathwick Mews garage, and he had a much more important partnership lined up with Katie. They were to be married in three months' time and had already put a deposit on a tumble-down cottage in rural Bucks where he would be able to work out his ambition to put old buildings into shape. It was ironic that Leo Selver's death should have led to his own chance of happiness. Buchanan had unpleasant memories of Trewartha Place and a permanent reminder of it in the shape of a scar above his right eyebrow, but these were unimportant while his relationship with Katie had given his life direction.

"Well, what's up, laddie?" Jack Collier, looking very spruce in a dark brown suit and cream shirt, was already on the bridge where they had planned to meet. There was no one else in sight and Collier called out his greetings in a loud voice. His tone was amiably negligent as if nothing could be much wrong on such a perfect day.

Buchanan walked up to him without saying anything and his answering grin was devoid of warmth. They shook hands and began to walk to and fro on the bridge, like the sentries pacing in front of Buckingham Palace.

"That inquest on Madoc . . ."

"Yes, Machin said you weren't happy about that. So for old times' sake, I looked into it. We've got to keep you happy, you see. Particularly now I hear you're joining the down-trodden majority. It's true what Machin said about the wedding bells?"

"Yes, early in the New Year. You'll get an invitation."

"Good." Collier stopped walking and took out his tobacco-pouch and pipe, going through the ritual in silence, dealing with it in unhurried thoroughness as he mentally dealt with the situation that had worried Buchanan. He pointed with his pipe at the antics of the moorhens, then said quietly: "That inquest in Launceston was concerned with the death of Madoc. Just that. The accidental death of one Richard Madoc, born of an illegitimate union in 1938, brought up in an orphanage in Plymouth, dishonourably discharged from the R.A.F. Police in 1970 with a dodgy record, the sole proprietor of Alpha Security. Madoc's dead, right? He died from misadventure. You're not going to argue about that?"

"Nothing was said ..."

"Nothing was said about a lot of things because there was no point in it." Collier had the tone of someone used to official sympathising and explaining. "Look, Madoc drove off a track into a bog. Right? You saw it and you tried your best to get him out. You skinned your hands badly on a rope pulling yourself out in the end. That was your story and everyone believed you. You were a good witness."

"It's being swept under the carpet."

"Rubbish. It isn't. Madoc's death was dealt with quite properly, due process of law, that sort of thing. It just wasn't the appropriate place to go into everything that Madoc may or may not have done. You believe that he killed Sidney Chard and that he may have been involved in the deaths of that young girl and your friend Leo Selver. You put it all together like a watch. You're probably right, though I doubt if we'd ever convince a jury. Madoc was clever, he didn't leave any dabs and he's not going to come back and give us a good cough. You think Mr. Chard and his Rover may be in that bog too. Probably right again, but we're not going to the expense of digging up that bloody morass to prove the point."

"I feel it's all being quietly dropped, filed away because of that list of names in the notebook. The list with 'Court-Card' on it. Because it might make trouble."

"Just not true. Selver and Chard can't be tried for blackmail because they're not around any more. Madoc can't be tried either ..."

"I'm not sure it was Madoc who did all of it. The man who attacked Freedson was wearing a mask."

"Doubts. Of course. That's what this business—my business —is about. Doubts, ifs, maybes. But it all makes good sense. Selver very foolishly got involved in this blackmailing lark but didn't have the nerve for it. He worried himself into thinking he was being followed, went to a private detective

156